THE URBANA FREE LIBRARY

W9-BCD-434

WHITE ELEPHANT

The Urbana Free Library

DISCARDED BY THE
URBANA FREE LIBRARY

To renew: call 217-367-4057
or go to **urbanafreelibrary.org**
and select **My Account**

COPYRIGHT 2016
by Juliet Winters Carpenter

PUBLISHED BY:
Chin Music Press Inc.
1501 Pike Place #329
Seattle, WA 98101
www.chinmusicpress.com

All rights reserved.

First (1) edition

COVER ART: *Winter Sphere* by Shingo Francis
COVER AND INTERIOR DESIGN: Mallory Jennings

Printed in the USA by Sheridan Books

LIBRARY OF CONGRESS CATALOGING-IN-PUBLICATION DATA:
Idemitsu, Mako, 1940-
Carpenter, Juliet Winters, translator
White Elephant
PL871.5.D46 H613 2016 | 895.63/6–dc23

PB ISBN 978-1-63405-958-9
EB ISBN 978-1-63405-959-6

WHITE ELEPHANT

a novel by MAKO IDEMITSU

Translated from the Japanese by Juliet Winters Carpenter

CHIN MUSIC
P R E S S

THE CHARACTERS

The Morimoto Family

MORIMASA	The Morimoto family patriarch
SADAKO	Wife of Morimasa; mother of the four sisters
HIROKO	Eldest daughter; artist; lives in New York City
EIKO	Second daughter
FUSAKO	Third daughter
SAKIKO	Fourth daughter; lives in Los Angeles with her son Hideto

Other Main Characters

SETSU	Sadako's mother
HANAKO	Sadako's younger sister
MISS YAMANE	Morimasa's secretary
MII-CHAN	Sakiko's childhood friend
RYOKO	Sakiko's friend from UCLA
PAUL	Sakiko's significant other
HIDETO	Sakiko and Paul's son
SHIZUKO	Hiroko's friend in New York
CHARLIE	Hiroko's significant other

1 The Girl Who Couldn't Say No

UCLA cafeteria, 1964.

The transparent sunlight of southern California highlighted the varied skin, hair, and eye colors of the people gathered beneath the high ceiling. People silently transporting forks and spoons to their mouths. People reaching for a coffee cup without taking their eyes off their book. People so absorbed in conversation they were forgetting to eat. Voices of laughter and amazement echoed against the glass walls.

Sakiko and Ryoko were sitting side by side on a sofa, drinking coffee. Poking a rip in the worn cushion with her finger, Sakiko wavered. Should she or shouldn't she say something about this weekend?

In front of them, a girl carrying textbooks and notebooks came by wearing a skirt with a design from kecak, the Balinese dance drama. "Nice skirt!" Ryoko called to her cheerfully. "That's kecak, right? Ever seen it?"

The girl broke into a smile. "Not yet! I mean to as soon as I get the chance."

Spurred by the eager voice of this person who seemed to expect her chance to emerge momentarily, Sakiko spoke up: "This weekend I'm going skydiving."

Ryoko shot her a look that was skeptical, then surprised. Skydivers, unlike theatergoers, risked death. "What? You mean you're going to do it?"

As Sakiko nodded timidly, Ryoko's gaze turned mocking. "All right, then tell me this. What is skydiving? Do you even know?"

"You jump out of an airplane, open your parachute, and land on the ground."

Ryoko's plump face reddened. "Have you practiced?"

Sakiko shook her head.

"And you still think you can do it?"

"Why not?"

"I asked if you still think you can do it."

"Matt and everybody said I could." Her voice was feeble.

"There's no way you can do it. You'll kill yourself!"

Listening to Ryoko shriek, Sakiko cringed at her inability to say no.

Memories of summer in Japan crossed her mind.

Sakiko's father, the business magnate Morimoto Morimasa, liked to wear *yukata*, light summer kimono. On the rare occasions when he ate at home in summer, he came to the table dressed in a *yukata* of bright indigo. Of course, that happened once or twice all summer, at most. Her mother Sadako, on the other hand, despised traditional Japanese clothing and always wore modern dresses. In other things she never violated her husband's express wishes, however unreasonable, but she never showed the slightest inclination to own a *yukata*. It was as if she bore the garment some resentment.

The four sisters—Hiroko, Eiko, Fusako, and Sakiko—were

never outfitted with *yukata*, whether their mother deliberately planned it that way or whether it was just too much trouble. Family lore had it that before they were married, she told Morimasa, "I loathe children." The care of the four girls was always left to maids.

Hiroko was Sakiko's elder by ten years, Eiko by seven. Those two each had a private maid, while Fusako and Sakiko, being just two years apart, always shared one. All four of them grew up in good health. Good physical health, anyway.

Sakiko had had trouble deciding what to do with herself after college. If she stayed in Japan she might well marry someone of whom her father approved, as Eiko and Fusako had done. The thought terrified her.

Lacking any brothers, the four sisters had had certain things drummed into them from the time they were old enough to listen—how their father had started his business without help from kith or kin, how he had struggled against adversity. The principle had been deeply impressed on each of them that it was their duty to devote themselves to him however they could, each in her own way.

Hiroko sought to enhance the prestige of her father's business in the cultural realm by succeeding as an artist. Eiko had done her bit by marrying, and Fusako had chosen marriage as well. Now it was Sakiko's turn. But something deep in Sakiko's nature repudiated marriage with the violence of a wave crashing on the shore. She had no rock-solid reason. As she was fretting over what to do, an acquaintance just back from the United States decided it for her: "Over there, it's taken for granted that kids leave home when they start college. Go to the States. Life there is fantastically free. You can take your time, think about what you want to do."

That same acquaintance had handled all the technical details connected with going to the US. Studying abroad was the quickest way to get a long-term visa, and he'd run around trying to arrange a scholarship for her, but with her grades that had proved impossible. Once again he had decided the next step: "There's nothing shameful about accepting help from your parents. You can always pay them back later."

After thinking up various excuses to win over her father, Sakiko had finally told him that she wanted to see American society because that's where the banks were that backed his business. It was almost too easy. He granted his approval.

"So Matt invited you."

Ryoko's eyes swam, as if she were dredging up a mental picture of the man.

Sakiko had once gone along with Matt, his wife, and their friends when they went skydiving. Matt had botched his landing and taken a bad spill. Fortunately, he survived with only injuries, but she'd overheard his wife mutter, "He'll kill himself yet." She'd blamed herself for failing to dissuade him from indulging in the risky sport, which struck Sakiko as pathetic. Yet when Matt said, "Next time it's your turn, Sakiko," she hadn't been able to say no.

"Why would you want to do something so dangerous?" Ryoko sounded like a scolding mother. In answer Sakiko slumped down, distraught. Her attitude must have conveyed the message that she wasn't keen on the idea.

"You don't want to do it!" Ryoko's eyes opened wide, bewilderment flying out of them. As her friend's wonder filled the space between them, Sakiko shook her head. No, she didn't want to do it.

"Then just say no!" Ryoko's tone was adamant. All of a sudden Sakiko felt as if she were being twisted and pulled. She wanted them to like her, Matt and Ryoko both. Now she'd gone and upset Ryoko. The thought that Ryoko might not like her anymore was painful and humiliating. She bent her head and wiped away the tears that came spilling out.

"Hi, Paul." Over her head Ryoko's voice chimed out, blithe and cheery again.

"Hi, Ryoko." The fellow named Paul came over, looked at Sakiko, who had raised her face, and did a double take. "It's you!" he said with a smile.

"You two know each other?" Ryoko said this with the relief of someone who had managed to escape from somewhere she didn't want to be.

"She was hitchhiking last week, and I picked her up." He spoke lightly, though something in his tone suggested there was cause for concern.

"Sakiko, you promised me you weren't going to hitchhike anymore!" Once again, Ryoko's tone was severe.

It had happened the day she went to a party at the invitation of Matt and his wife. Those two took off early, and she'd fled to escape the attentions of a man who might have gotten annoying if she'd let him see her home; but there was no public transportation and she hadn't had cab fare, so hitchhiking had been her only choice.

Paul glanced at Sakiko, his pale blue eyes shining sharply, framed by shoulder-length blond hair, before turning again to Ryoko: "I was coming back from a swim in Malibu, on Pacific Coast Highway, and saw this young lady standing by the side of the road, tottering. One look and I could tell she was high. I don't pick up hitchhikers as a rule, but I just couldn't leave her standing there."

"This young lady doesn't know how to take care of herself. Why, just now…" She told the story of Sakiko's inability to turn down the skydiving invitation.

Paul studied Sakiko as if she were some sort of bizarre

creature, the blue of his eyes deepening as she watched.

"Well, Ryoko, if she can't tell him no, why don't you do it for her?"

"No thanks. I've done enough. I've looked out for her all I'm going to." Lips pursed, she looked at Sakiko and said snappishly with a toss of her head, "If you have a mind to do this, go right ahead. Kill yourself, nobody's stopping you."

Ryoko had married a Japanese American she met in Tokyo, moved to Los Angeles with him, and, when their only daughter started taking up less of her time, began auditing classes at UCLA—just as she and her husband had promised each other she would do, twelve years ago on the boat from Japan.

Soon after Sakiko came to the university to study English as a foreign language, she had entered the cafeteria for the first time. She'd stood around helplessly until Ryoko came up to her, said briskly, "You from Japan?" and helped her get in line. Ryoko had taken food from the counter, making demands of the workers on the other side—"Have you got some of that? Then would you do this?"—all the while chattering away: "I had my first class today. It was great. How about you?" Her friendly gaze was dazzling.

That was two years ago. Still Sakiko's only friend, she was also her substitute mother.

"I'll do it then," said Paul.

"Would you?"

Listening to them talk, Sakiko buried her face in Ryoko's ample bosom. The tips of Ryoko's fingers stroked her head and occasionally patted her lightly, as if to say *Sorry I scared you.* Gradually, she relaxed. Though she didn't consciously realize that in addition to the mother figure of Ryoko, now the father figure of Paul had appeared, she felt a vague sense of relief.

Her life was controlled by the habit of leaving things to others, as it had been ever since she could remember.

"Crackers, caramels!"

When the first movie ended and intermission started, the candy-seller's voice resounded through the theater. When she came near where ten-year-old Sakiko was sitting, she took a box of caramels from the big box of snacks that she wore slung around her neck and laid it on Sakiko's lap with a warm smile. Though she had no money, Sakiko reached for her pocket, but the lady patted her on the hand and said softly, "My treat. Thanks for always buying something." Then she straightened up and walked off, calling, "Crackers, caramels!"

The night before, Sakiko's father hadn't come home, so she hadn't been able to slip a bill from his wallet like always. Instead she'd waited till her mother came home drunk late at night, rummaged in the pockets of her cast-off garments, and managed to scrounge the price of a ticket.

As far as sneaking money from their parents' wallets went, the two younger sisters had a tacit understanding: Sakiko would take money from their father, Fusako from their mother. For Fusako, ill-treating her little sister was less a pleasure than a purpose in life, but in this one matter, perhaps because Sakiko had first caught her stealing, she was magnanimous.

I bet the candy lady could tell I'm broke. Joy in having someone take an interest in her came springing up all the way from her toes, tucked inside hand-me-down shoes from Fusako; her hands shook so hard that she could hardly get the box of caramels open.

In second grade she'd been home alone one day when a family friend came by and took her to the movie theater. That was her very first time. Though the theater wasn't close, the distance from home was walkable, so she got in the habit of rushing over after school as soon as she changed her clothes.

When she stood in line, the grownups in front of her cut off her view; then the person in front of her would suddenly disappear and she'd be at the ticket office. On tiptoe, she'd say, "One child, please." When the ticket girl saw her, she'd grin and say, "Hiya! Back again?" That made Sakiko happy.

She soon learned to go to the bathroom after getting her seat. Pressed between men jangling steel pinballs in their pockets and perfumed women who worked in snack bars at night, Sakiko stared intently at the screen, her short legs dangling above the floor. Most of the time she didn't know what was going on, but she could tell when the heroine had to marry a person of her parents' choosing even though she loved someone else. *I'll never get married that way.* Without her realizing it, the conviction grew in her heart. The theater she'd been going to for several years showed only Japanese movies, love stories with sad endings. Women who mopped their tears with a hanky, not caring if their makeup got smeared, would emerge looking cheered and hurry off to their evening's work.

When she left the movie theater, Sakiko would stop by a fruit parlor. Surrounded by grownups who smoked cigarettes and talked in loud voices, she would eat a parfait and pray that whoever she married would give her something this good to eat every day. Here too she became a familiar figure and was treated to extra dollops of whipped cream. Nobody was waiting at home to eat supper with her, but if she was late she felt sorry for the maid, who doubled as cook, so mostly she went home as early as she could.

One time, Sakiko told the mother of her friend Mii-chan, who lived in the same neighborhood, about going to the movies. "You go see grownup movies like that all by yourself?" Mii-chan's mother had said in surprise, stopping her sewing. "Why, I'm surprised your mother lets you!"

Mii-chan's mother worked at home as a seamstress. Her

work was always careful; when she altered something, for example, she would sew on patches of lovely material. "I thought I might do it this way. What do you think?" Not pushy, she would show clients her ideas with a mixture of confidence and shyness. Sakiko had been around for this any number of times. When the client was pleased, it made Sakiko so happy that she'd do a little jig, making the grownups smile. The arrangements of little cloths that Mii-chan's mother came up with were refreshing and elegant and full of consideration for the wearer, like Mii-chan's mother herself. That was why people liked them and gave her so much business, Sakiko thought.

The little house where Mii-chan lived with her parents had escaped the war fires, but patch it up though they would, it kept springing leaks. Whenever that happened, Mii-chan's mother would get out empty cans and bottles she collected for the purpose and set them where the raindrops fell, enjoying the sounds they made. "Listen," she'd say, "what do you think? Isn't that a lovely, transparent sound?"

Mii-chan's mother fed Sakiko delicious suppers made with vegetables she grew in her tiny, postage stamp garden; she also checked Sakiko's homework and listened to her chatter. Sakiko went home only to sleep, forgetful now of the maid who doubled as a cook. In Sakiko's heart, Mii-chan's family felt more like family than her own.

Sakiko never talked to her mother about going to the movies. Mother and daughter never talked, period. As long as no one pointed fingers at her daughter, Sadako was unconcerned. Whether anyone was in fact pointing fingers, she didn't trouble herself to learn. In any case, Sakiko had trouble thinking of herself as Sadako's "daughter"; the word itself didn't seem real.

She used to go to the amusement park with Fusako, but once she got old enough, she went by herself. It was a nice change from Fusako criticizing every little thing she did, from

15

her choice of ride to the way she rode on things and enjoyed herself; it was a nice change from having her sister act like she was doing her a big favor by taking her at all.

After a thrilling ride, other kids carried on, whooping in excitement and running to their grownups while she slipped past them frowning and trying to decide which ride to go on next. *Hmf, they're silly to be so scared,* she would think, a mixture of scorn and envy on her face. The amusement park staff were also nice to her and sometimes shared their lunch.

Sakiko got used to doing things alone—being alone was easy and natural—but she was lonely. It delighted her whenever anyone took an interest in her or was nice to her, anyone at all. The thought of offending someone or earning their dislike, on the other hand, was terrifying. To keep that from ever happening, she learned to adapt. The habit of never saying no became deeply ingrained.

The marinated chicken dropped into the hot oil in the wok with a sizzle. The sound sparkled, reflecting Sakiko's feelings.

Several months had gone by since she and Paul had crossed paths in the UCLA cafeteria. Sakiko had moved into his studio-cum-residence, a former shop in a beachside shopping district that was home to a large colony of artists.

Tonight she would be hostess for the first time. They were having six people over, all close friends. A casual dinner party. As she set the table, she softly sang Sakamoto Kyu's song "*Ue o muite aruko,*" which had become popular in the US as "Sukiyaki Song." *I look up as I walk / So the tears won't fall / Remembering spring days / This lonely night.*

Except when she came to the last line, she changed it to "Not lonely now." Laughter came bubbling up irrepressibly. As she set out the Shigaraki and Bizen wares she'd brought over from Japan, Paul's cries of admiration—"Great!" "Wow!"—bounced off the ceiling.

Slices of sashimi, *harusame* noodle salad, a bowl of colorful *chirashizushi* rice salad, and a platter of fried chicken flavored with ginger, garlic, and soy sauce were arranged on the table. As Paul's arms circled her from behind and slid inside her jeans, he and she kissed, looked at the table, and kissed again, all smiles. Ryoko, just back from Japan, was going to bring over some fresh wasabi. Paul had only ever eaten powdered wasabi before, and the thought of what he would say when he tasted the real thing was exciting. Every time she taught him something new about Japan he exclaimed with pleasure; if he ever started tiring of it, what would she do?

Paul released her and disappeared into the bathroom, and she checked the position of the knives and forks. At the touch of the cold silverware her heart lurched, and she shivered. As she was rearranging some chopsticks, her fingers went rigid and trembled, so the chopsticks fell. Sudden fear that she might fail in her role as hostess made her heart weaken; her body felt as if it might give way, crumbling from the feet up. She wanted to vanish. The thought of the doorbell ringing was terrifying.

When had he come back? Paul squeezed her tightly from behind and whispered, "It's okay. The food you make tastes great, and you're good at entertaining people. You're a terrific hostess. The only one who doesn't know it is you. Stop worrying."

She felt as if she were in the arms of a father as gentle as a mother. *Is it true? Really?* she asked wordlessly as, reverting to childhood, she pounded his arm, sniffed, and peered up into his face, shaking her head petulantly. "It's okay," he said, rocking her gently. "Let it all out." Wrapped in his warmth, supported and protected, she felt her feet slowly touch the ground, until finally she could stand firm.

As she tested the almond pudding to make sure it was done, Paul said softly, as if checking her emotional state, "It's like there are two Sakikos. Sometimes that's the way it seems."

"How do you mean?"

"Well, for starters," he said mildly, after checking to be sure she wasn't still shaky on her feet, "there's the Sakiko who waits calmly for me when I'm late, swinging her leg, and smiling when she sees me. Then there's the Sakiko who turns pale with fear when I'm late, worried I might not show up, ready to burst with anxiety. At one party she'll go around meeting people, talking to them and enjoying herself, and at another party just as informal she'll tense up and go all quiet. There's the Sakiko who sees a friend at the supermarket and calls out a cheery hello, and the one who can't do that to save her life, not even to the same friend. Everybody gets depressed now and then. Everybody has times when they can't seem to rise to the occasion. But with you it seems different. I sense something deep-rooted. Nothing severe enough to interfere with daily life, but still."

Yes, let's call that other girl "Yuko," written with the character for "excellence." Sakiko had named her that herself. Unlike Sakiko, Yuko was excellent. A girl her imagination dreamed up. On her way to and from school, the amusement park, or the movie theater, she would imagine her. Yuko was Sakiko's same age. Every year they had their birthday together. Yuko was cheerful and open, universally liked, praised for whatever she did. A girl of confidence and courage, she was smart enough to know what she should and shouldn't do. She could take action when action was needed, speak up clearly, present herself well. She was Sakiko's opposite in every possible way. Everything that Sakiko lacked, Yuko had.

When no one was home, Sakiko would sit at a round table drawing Yuko on sheet after sheet of calligraphy practice paper. Yuko had a straight back and an intelligent face with big dark eyes and a happy, relaxed smile. Sakiko would pick up a drawing, press it to her cheek, and murmur, "Yuko is me, I am Yuko."

Sitting in the train one time, Sakiko was smiling to herself, happily imagining a scene in which Yuko won praise, when a middle-aged woman in the seat across from her gave her a funny look. Wishing to share her happiness with the woman, Sakiko smiled at her, and the woman smiled back, apparently deciding that the little girl in front of her must be enjoying some pleasant memory. That was as far as Sakiko's inner Yuko came out.

Suddenly, Yuko vanished. Seized by shame and regret, Sakiko let her head drop. She shrank into herself, clenching her hands into fists on top of the school satchel resting on her knees. She felt as if not only the woman with whom she had just exchanged glances but everyone in the car must be looking at her curiously. Her chest tightened. She could hardly breathe. With her every muscle frozen, she couldn't get off the train. It was the Yamanote Line, so the train kept circling around and around.

When Fusako was teasing her, Sakiko would pray for Yuko to come, but she never did. She was always away somewhere. Only after Sakiko had taken a thorough beating and was reduced to nothing would Yuko finally appear. The barbs that Fusako flung at her—a disgrace to the family; a foundling deserted by a prostitute; a stupid, hopeless idiot—ripped into her heart, leaving gaping wounds; but Yuko would touch her lips gently to each hurt and make it better.

Sakiko drew picture after picture of Yuko, a dazzling figure receiving rounds of applause. She changed the color of her dress each time, red to yellow to pink, and signed each sketch "Yuko." She tried to give each figure the same expression, with sparkling eyes that looked up at her admirers with mixed embarrassment and pride, but it was hard. She would do it over but eventually tear the paper by pushing too hard, feeling as if she herself were the target of praise. She used only bright colors, so those crayons got used up fast.

Oh no. Someone was coming. Better hurry and clean up. Mother wouldn't be home this early, before supper. If it was Hiroko, she'd go straight to her room without ever noticing Sakiko, let alone the table. If it was Eiko, she'd scold, "Cut that out and do your homework." If it was Fusako, she'd tease her mercilessly day and night for a week.

"Selling his works doesn't bring in enough for us to live on, so Paul's teaching college."

Hiroko responded with a snort of derision.

Sakiko was visiting Hiroko at her place in New York. An apartment building in Manhattan's exclusive residential district, with a uniformed doorman standing guard at the entrance.

"Father's paying your way..." Sakiko looked around, the words sticking in her throat. From just inside the entryway you could see the kitchen with its row of appliances—a big refrigerator, a dishwasher, an oven—and the living room with a leather sofa. There was a big room with windows that Hiroko used as a studio, and another room that she called her "guest room" but that looked to Sakiko like storage space for her artwork. Further back was the bedroom, with warm carpeting and special-order thick curtains to keep out the light. There were two bathrooms and a powder room.

After graduating from college, Hiroko had declined all offers of an arranged marriage and wedded someone she herself brought home, announcing brusquely, "No way I'm ever having kids, all right?" A few years later she'd divorced her husband and moved to New York. Their father was paying her living expenses on the understanding that she would become a successful artist.

Hiroko watched her baby sister surveying the inside of the condo. It seemed to her that ever since she'd started living with an artist, Sakiko had got the idea she herself was an artist. The little idiot. From the minute she arrived, she'd been bombarding Hiroko with stupid questions like "Why don't you live in a loft like other people?" She began every other sentence with "Paul says...." Living in a loft didn't make you an artist. You became an artist by producing works of art, works that other people valued. Living in this neighborhood meant she didn't have to spend time worrying about safety and could focus on her painting. The idea of a loft in Soho was terrifying; she couldn't possibly live in such a place.

During the war when she was sent to work in an airplane factory—one of many students pressed into factory work by order of the Ministry of Education, to compensate for the labor shortage—Hiroko had trembled in fear alongside her friend Yuriko. After a while when the sirens went off and an air raid got underway, Yuriko would shriek and writhe in agony. Hiroko had wanted to join in, but she couldn't. People used to feel sorry for Yuriko, figuring she'd lost her wits, but Hiroko had felt envious. Since she was little she had formed the habit of controlling her emotions, and perhaps for that reason she was unable to cry.

When she was still married, once while she was lying in bed, unwell, her husband had struck and knocked down a girlfriend who'd come by to see her. Hearing her friend fight back fiercely, she had fainted dead away. When Hiroko sought to escape from something happening in reality, her consciousness would dim. Escape was the means of self-defense she had acquired in the process of growing up. After that, whenever something similar happened, she would unconsciously resort to the technique of fainting.

"You know what? Paul says I should take in some jazz while I'm here in New York. There's some great performer called John Coltrane who's on stage now, he says. He was all jealous, said he wished he could go. Shall we? Since he made such a point of it, I'd feel bad not to."

I can't let him down, I'll hurt his feelings, he'll get mad... Sakiko kept driving the point home, and in the end she and Hiroko headed for a Broadway club called Birdland.

The cabbie glanced at the address scribbled on a sheet of memo paper and looked at the two of them disapprovingly. When they got out, he admonished them, "Ladies, watch yourselves." The manager seemed taken aback at the sight of two women without escorts and ushered them to a table directly in front of the stage where they seated themselves, conscious of coming under the concentrated fire of everyone's gaze.

"Hi, ladies!" As soon as they were settled, a breezy waiter came along to take their order. Sakiko ordered a drink, and Hiroko said "I'll have the same," not knowing what it might be. To distract herself she looked at the piano off to the left and reflected on the trivial fact that it was only a couple of steps away. She didn't want Sakiko to sense her fear and have word of it get out to their sisters, robbing her of her carefully nurtured stature among the four of them.

A black man came out holding a sax. Sakiko whispered,

"That must be him." The room was suddenly abuzz with anticipation.

What was happening? Something like a whirlwind had risen inside Hiroko. Her soul was gripped tight and twisted. A welter of buried emotions came up from the recesses of her heart. She called on all her reserves of knowledge to resist, but was overwhelmed. *I'm scared! Don't touch me.*

Sadness came bubbling up. This was what Hiroko most wished to avoid—having her feelings engaged. Feelings were unpleasant. Back during the war, people had let their feelings run rampant and charged forward, saying it was all for the country's sake. Let the nation fight as one, they'd said, but all that idealism didn't win the war. "Be a compassionate person of deep feeling," their father Morimasa used to instruct the family, and they'd all listened respectfully. But Hiroko despised feelings, didn't trust them. What counted more was reason. Reason was a weapon.

My paintings, when someone like Sakiko with no understanding sees them, apparently look like nothing more than gobs of paint, something even a monkey could do; but they are backed by thought and logic. To release the indignation welling up inside her, Hiroko clapped furiously.

Sakiko looked at Hiroko and saw fear in her expression. What could it mean? Meanwhile Coltrane went on playing, with no apparent regard for the beat. His eyes were the universe. The three of them were each lost in their own world, in some strange way. Since she and Hiroko were the only two listening, why didn't he just call it a night?

When the music finally ended, her sister's cheeks were streaked with tears. Having never seen her sister cry before, much less in a place like this, Sakiko felt something inside jerk. A peculiar feeling.

The next morning Sakiko awoke to the sound of a husky voice over her head: "Rise and shine, sleeping beauty!" A plump black woman in a white uniform was looking down at her with a friendly smile.

"I want to sleep some more," Sakiko said petulantly.

"You a lady, ain't you? Get up and get yourself dressed!" The woman snatched off her covers.

Smiling despite herself at the idea of treating a lady's bed-covers with such lack of ceremony, Sakiko got up. She envied Hiroko for waking into this warmth every day.

She sat down with Hiroko to a brunch that the woman had made while singing a Negro spiritual in ringing tones. "She's great," she said. "A real earth mother."

Hiroko leaned her head a bit to one side and said in a shy murmur, "She's what keeps me alive."

Ever since last night Hiroko had been acting strange, weeping while listening to Coltrane, and now this. "This omelet's amazing," Sakiko said, changing the subject. She was aware of the look of sadness on her sister's face, accompanied by a chill loneliness, but such things made her go stiff, put her at a loss for words. It was all she could do to escape. She wanted only to be free of the snare of her own loneliness.

With her left hand Sakiko turned the pages of the textbook for the college entrance exam while with her right hand she plied her chopsticks. Ever since Fusako went away to college, Sakiko had been eating alone. Her best friend Mii-chan had gone to work in an office, and since entering high school Sakiko had found it awkward to visit the house where she used to spend so much time. If she did go they'd be glad to see her, she suspected, but somewhere inside a voice whispered, "People like you aren't popular." Today she really wanted to stop by on the way home from school, but at the turning place once again she heard that inner voice. In response her body turned toward home.

But this time she resisted, letting her feet carry her forward. When Mii-chan's mother came to the front door, spotted her standing there, embraced her with a shout of joy, snug in those arms she cried her eyes out.

Back when she went to Mii-chan's house regularly, she'd once told Mii-chan's mother, "I'm lonesome 'cause my father and mother are never home."

"That sounds very lonesome," Mii-chan's mother had said. "I can well imagine. But you know, ever since the war ended, it hasn't been easy just getting enough to eat. Your father works hard so you don't have to go hungry. When you get lonesome, come on over to our house." Her hair was pulled tight, showing the marks of the comb, and she had on a white apron. Sakiko snuggled against her, and she stroked Sakiko's head gently while she spoke.

Remembering those words had kept her going, but now Fusako was out so much of the time that Sakiko was more lonesome than ever. Even a sister like Fusako would be nice to have around.

As she was arranging the pleated skirt of her school uniform so it would be pressed into shape beneath her futon while she slept, the front door opened. Who was home first tonight? Her mother's rough, drunken voice called, "Tae! Tae!" and the maid Taeko came tearing out of her room beside the kitchen. Poor thing. She could only take her bath and go to bed after everyone else. In the morning she was the first one up. In the beginning her cheeks had been pink and she'd answered brightly when called, but now she was pale and listless, her voice muffled. Still, every time a letter came from her mother in the countryside, her cheeks would turn pink again and laughter poured out of her. That made Sakiko jealous.

In a while Eiko came home. To get to her room she had to come through Sakiko's room, and as she went past her futon she smiled at her and said "I'm back," as if discharging a duty. "Welcome back," Sakiko responded, and started to say something about her day, but Eiko slid the door to her room shut without a backward glance, as if to say, "Sorry, some other time."

When Sakiko heard Fusako come home, she could hardly wait for her to slip into the futon next to hers. As she lay waiting expectantly, the door flew open and Fusako slid under the covers with a "G'night." And then, signaling "I'm tired, don't talk to me," turned her back.

"You're pregnant."

When the doctor told her this, superimposed on his face she'd seen that of Morimasa, her father. Warmth so great it made you want to trust him with everything, accompanied by intimidating strength of will.

Sakiko lingered on the beach, before her the Pacific Ocean and beyond it the land where her father lived, Japan. She came here nearly every day, but she'd never thought of it that way before.

Her thoughts swayed back and forth as the dazzling sun beat down.

She wouldn't have the child. But if she went back to Japan for an abortion, she probably couldn't come back to the States. She would have neither the money nor the courage.

"Sakiko!"

A shout loud enough to rattle her brain. Paul put his arms around her from behind. "What did the doctor say?"

She only bit her lip hard and looked into his blue eyes, fuzzy in the strong sunlight. Moments passed as he waited for her answer. Then she saw his eyes were shining. His voice sounded again, full of excitement.

"You're having our baby. Right?"

As Paul's hand stole out to touch her belly, she resisted the impulse to grab it and throw it aside. The message her mother had conveyed since the time Sakiko floated in amniotic fluid was engraved in the bottom of her heart: "Having a child is the beginning of a woman's unhappiness."

"When I didn't hear from you, I canceled class and came home," Paul went on, looking mildly down at Sakiko's forbidding face. "I know you're wavering. You're only with me to defy your daddy, anyway."

Daddy? Who would that be, her father? Daddy, Father…the gap between the two words made her dizzy. If Morimasa ever heard her call him such a thing he would probably explode: "What kind of a name is that to call your parent!" And after he'd gone out of earshot, Eiko and Fusako would dissolve in laughter: "Daddy! Did you ever?" Then they would sigh, "Laughed so hard my side hurts," and suddenly cast unfriendly looks at her, Sakiko.

"I won't force you. If you don't want it, I won't say anything."

As she stood there, alternately warmed by the heat of the sun and cooled by the chill ocean breeze, Paul's soothing words hung in the air.

On a screen of white clouds overhead, ringed in rosy light, she saw an image of her sister Fusako holding her firstborn, whom she'd given birth to last year. She looked at Sakiko with an air of triumph and said provokingly, "Well, Sakiko? Aren't you jealous?" Beside her appeared Hiroko, exuding lonely desolation in New York. Bleeding through these images was her fear of losing Paul. One reason for his divorce, he'd told her, was his ex-wife's inability to have children.

One time before she met Paul, when she was living alone in a little apartment in Westwood, she'd made grilled saury for dinner. It was frozen, something she'd bought at a Japanese grocery store. Rays of setting sun lit up the blue-black back of the fish where it lay on the table beside wallpaper so crowded with gaudy flowers that it might have been a vision of either heaven or hell. Just before sunset, the sun's rays were especially intense, with insidious strength. The half-cooked fish's eyes, tinged with red, were saying something to her. Telling her there was something it forgot to take with it to the world below.

She'd felt a vague presentiment all that day. It seemed to her that something her own ancestors had failed to take with them to the grave was calling secretly to whatever it was the saury had failed to take with it. Her whole body vibrated, as if a light electric current were passing through her. The phone rang. She jumped up, picked up the receiver, and said, "Junk speaking." While the caller searched for a response, she hung up. The phone rang again. She didn't pick it up after that.

"Walk! Walk! Don't go to sleep! Keep your eyes open!"

A man's loud voice sounded in her ear. People were holding her up on either side, forcing her to walk. She was sleepy, horribly sleepy. How wonderful it would be if they stopped holding her up so she could sink to the floor and go back to sleep.

"Walk! Walk!"

"Walk, Sakiko. You've got to keep walking."

This was a woman's voice. Whose? She'd heard it somewhere

before. For an instant her mind cleared, and she murmured, "Ryoko…" Then the fog returned. When she tripped and fell, they pulled her to her feet and poured water down her throat.

"Drink up. Drink a lot." Ryoko's stern voice. Sakiko burped and turned her face away in disgust, but someone slapped her. "Drink it!" This happened over and over.

Ryoko spoke to her without cease. "In the movie *The Third Man* a cat comes out and winds itself around Harry's legs, and that's how we know the man whose legs are all we can see is Harry, remember?" This was a scene Sakiko had often talked about with pleasure. "We saw somebody who looked like Orson Welles, the man who played Harry, walking down Hollywood Boulevard on his way to a car, and we got all excited thinking it might be him, remember?"

"Uh-huh," responded Sakiko, and started to fall asleep again. "Just let me lie down." As she struggled to get the words out, Ryoko's sweat-soaked face froze in a look that was bloodcurdling. Memories came back of her father, Morimasa. As she came to, the contents of her stomach came churning up.

"Once she throws up, she'll be fine." This was a man's deep voice, evidently a doctor.

Worried when, after hanging up with the words "Junk speaking," Sakiko hadn't answered the phone, Ryoko had let herself in with her key and found Sakiko lying asleep next to an empty bottle of sleeping pills.

Somewhere in the neighborhood a party must be going on; the streets were lined with cars parked bumper to bumper. Sakiko parked several blocks away. *Who's throwing a party? Why weren't Paul and I invited?*

She opened the studio door. Waves of sound pounded and reverberated against the concrete walls. Before her eyes was a crowd of people, head after head of blond and brown hair. The smell of white people filled the room. She faltered. The next moment, through the hubbub she heard Paul's voice calling her name.

"Sakiko!"

His sparkling eyes had been on the lookout for her. This was a surprise party of some kind, but what was it for? And who? Paul pushed his way through the crowd and appeared in front of her, wearing a suit for a change. "Welcome home," he said, giving her a light kiss, and led her on into the room.

Shrimp cocktail, roast beef, deviled eggs: an array of fancy party foods. A gorgeous flower arrangement was at the back wall, and in front of it stood Paul's friend Shawn, also wearing a suit for once. Normally dour-faced and stingy with smiles, today he greeted them with a beaming face. *So this is what he looks like when he smiles,* Sakiko was thinking bemusedly, when somehow she found herself standing facing him with Paul at her side. Someone behind her handed her a bouquet of flowers. "Thank you," she said automatically. (Since coming to this country, she had acquired the habit of saying "thank you" on all occasions; even once after someone ran into her car, when they parted she'd said, "Thank you.") She turned around to see who it was, and there stood Ryoko, all dressed up. Surprise and relief filled her. "Hey, what's going on?" she said, and Ryoko grabbed her by the shoulder and pushed her back to face Shawn. At her friend's no-nonsense attitude Sakiko turned back reluctantly, like a daughter yielding to her mother.

With a shake of his long blond ponytail, like a horse flicking its tail, Shawn opened a book bound in black leather and began to read aloud some words that made no sense to Sakiko. Then he solemnly asked Paul something again incomprehensible. When Paul answered "Yes," Shawn directed the same inquiry to her. The blue eyes in his pale face stared at her so hard that she shuddered.

Sweeping back her dirty hair, the lady came and went from the garage where she lived, using a single bucket for all her needs. She did her laundry in it, washed her dishes in it, even relieved herself in it during the night. In the morning she would carry the malodorous bucket through the garage side door to empty it, paying no attention when its contents splashed on her. Apparently there was a toilet there that she was allowed to use in the daytime.

The lady sat on a strong-looking box with something written on it in big letters of the alphabet, laid a big plate on her lap and ate scraps from the American family living over the garage. She used a knife and fork, items that the American family had perhaps thrown away, the motions of her hands so graceful that five-year-old Sakiko, watching from a second-floor window across the way, was mesmerized. Sakiko was just back from having been evacuated during the war, and knives and forks by themselves were something special in her eyes let alone the elegance with which the lady wielded them. Peering from the bottom of the window, Sakiko's face gradually turned upward. The lady daintily raised a chipped cup to her lips. Clothes resembling cleaning rags hung drying on a cord strung across the garage entrance, filling the air with a sour smell.

When Sakiko went by the garage, she ran past it on the opposite side of the street. Terror was of course the reason; besides, she did not want to catch lice and have to be sprayed with DDT until she turned white. The lady's swollen body was covered with filthy rags. Her age was indeterminable. It was as if, perhaps from living like a domestic animal, all trace of her age had been obliterated.

After the war, an American family stationed in Japan had requisitioned the charming white Western-style house that had survived the fire-bombs, forcing the lady, its owner, to move out to the garage. The new occupants were a white married couple with a daughter and son around the age of ten. The family came and went in a black chauffeured car. The father and children left the house together every morning. In the afternoon, when the children came home they would race up the stone steps, the girl's bouncing blonde hair tied in a colorful ribbon and the boy's flying legs encased in shorts and lace-up boots, and disappear behind the solid front door. They might have been urging people ahead of them: "The outside's crawling with viruses. Hurry, run for your life!" Even in that brief interval, Sakiko was entranced by the gaiety they scattered as they ran and by the cleanliness of their fair, well-nourished skin—skin so fair that it seemed to deflect the rays of the sun. Her father sometimes brought home a bar of Hershey's chocolate, and that same sweet fragrance rose from the house, the smell of longing and bliss.

The mother appeared only when she was going out somewhere. She always wore a hat pulled low and descended the steps with her face turned down. To get from the bottommost step into the car, she had to place one foot in the street, which she did by touching only the toe of her high heel to the ground and bounding lightly inside the vehicle; it appeared she was trying to minimize her contact with the street so as to prevent infection. A Japanese maid would come out to see her off, wearing a black uniform and a white apron with edging, on her head a cloth cap with the same edging. When the car bearing her mistress turned the corner, the maid would run straight back up the steps lest a passer-by speak to her.

There was a cook, too. Just once Sakiko saw him leaving by the side door. He was a thin, middle-aged Japanese man, and he too walked quickly with his head bent down to avoid eye contact with people. He never went shopping in the neighborhood, as all the household food and other goods were imported from America. The lady in the garage used an empty can of pineapple for a serving dish; what was left of the photograph on it shone a bright yellow.

The Western-style building was tightly shut and admitted no one. Heavy curtains were always drawn at the windows facing the street. No sounds emerged. But the place had a silent, intimidating air that filled people outside with dread.

The cook and the maid were forbidden to speak to the lady in the garage. While their employer was traveling, the maid had suffered unbearable pain from toothache and scurried to the dentist, where she revealed this tidbit. By the candy store Sakiko overheard neighbors talking about it. As the house's former resident, the lady was of course known in the neighborhood, but what had become of her relations to other people little Sakiko had no way of knowing. Yet young though she was, she could sense that grownups had all they could do to manage their own lives, and no energy to spare for others.

One day as she was walking past the garage, Sakiko watched as the side door opened and an arm came out, setting a can on the floor. The lady who normally ate so elegantly from a large plate scuttled over like an animal, scooped up the contents of the can with her fingers and stuffed it in her mouth. Seeing this, Sakiko recoiled and stood still. Her blood ran cold, as if she had seen something horrific. Hastily she tried to run off and tripped, skinning her knee. It hurt so much she wanted to cry, but she couldn't. One person feeding another like an animal. The moment the light coming from behind the open door lit up the dark concrete space, the cruelty of it hit her, shutting off even the possibility of tears.

How many days went by after that? The lady's voice, once a mumble, gradually grew louder and fiercer until she was ranting, and then she started strewing excrement from the bucket into the street; and then she disappeared.

Remembering, Sakiko shook with fright. When her body stopped shaking, the tremors in her heart went on. She wanted someone to know. But everyone in her family acted as if the lady had never existed. Her family never talked to begin with, so she was unable to bring it up. She tried once to talk to Eiko about the lady, but was turned aside with a grimace. Fusako shouted at her, "Shut up!"

And so Sakiko's terror stayed inside her, fermenting, and clung to the walls of her heart like mold. Mixed in with it was her dread of the lady's madness, and of white people as conquerors not to be resisted.

Shawn's blue eyes, surrounded by pale skin, were turned piercingly on Sakiko. Pinned by his gaze, she couldn't move a muscle. Her blood turned to ice.

"Yes," she was saying.

As cheers erupted, Paul put his hand on her stiff face and drew it closer, then kissed her expressionless lips. After that he slipped a ring on her finger. Though her hands were rigid, she managed to do the same to his.

His colleague Alice gave them liquid-filled glasses. Following Paul's lead, Sakiko turned to face everyone. All around were white arms holding up wine glasses. "To the happy couple!" Shouts resounded on all sides. Yet again, the smell of white people as conquerors. Feeling as if from the top of her head to the tips of her toes she was filled with a snarl of thread, with a trembling hand Sakiko downed whatever was in the glass. Champagne.

"Now throw your bouquet. Turn around, throw it over your head!"

Urged on by Ryoko's voice, Sakiko lifted the bedraggled bouquet of flowers in her hand, taken evidently from the garden of the person living behind them, and tossed it into the air.

The bouquet rose listlessly and plopped into the hands of Dan, a gay guy who'd graduated from Harvard at the top of his class. His boyfriend had just left him and he'd been feeling down, but now people flocked around him with congratulations.

And so, just like that, Sakiko was married.

Though advised by Paul and her friends that she needed to tell her parents she'd gotten married, Sakiko felt a tightness in her chest at the mere thought of doing so. At least write them a letter, people said, but her body seized up.

"Some kind of a daughter you are," said Ryoko. "Okay, okay. I'm going back next month, so I'll go see them and tell them for you."

Yay! Wonderful! Inside Sakiko shouted with joy, although Paul fixed her with a stern look.

According to the report Ryoko gave, as soon as she arrived she had phoned Sakiko's mother, Sadako. "One moment, please," said the girl who helped around the house, and apparently went off to summon her mistress. Then the same voice said, "Madam has gone out."

"When will she be back?"

"I...don't know."

No matter how many times she was made to do it, the girl never got used to lying, apparently. Ryoko had left the number where she was staying, but no one ever contacted her. Next she'd phoned Sakiko's father, Morimasa, at his company, and his secretary, Miss Yamane—the sound of her name warmed Sakiko's heart—had promptly set up an appointment.

That day, as she was sitting nervously in the reception room, Morimasa had come up and thanked her sincerely for befriending his daughter, finishing with a respectful bow of the head. He was utterly unlike the intimidating man she'd imagined. After she got back to California, Ryoko reenacted the scene and clutched her sides with laughter. "Really, it was too much!"

On hearing that Sakiko had married a white artist named Paul, Morimasa had shown no surprise. "Is that right? So she got married, did she?" He had then looked out the window reflectively, silent for a few moments. Emboldened by his calmness, Ryoko had told him about the pregnancy as well. A fierce light gleamed in his eyes, and Ryoko was afraid she might have gone too far, but her fears proved unfounded. Quickly reverting to an expression of such tenderness that anyone would have been charmed, he said quietly, "Is that so? She's having a baby?" After that he had spoken of his economic philosophy, and never brought up Sakiko's name again. When she left, he bowed his head again and said, "My daughter has a stubborn streak, but she needs a friend like you."

When Miss Yamane saw Ryoko off, she had handed her one envelope marked "Carfare" and another, filled with money, that she'd said was for Sakiko.

"He's on a totally different scale from other people. So masculine. Such a great man."

Sakiko had been amazed to hear her friend go on about her father in this way.

Shortly after the call Ryoko paid on Morimasa, a letter from Eiko had arrived.

> *Father told us about your marriage and pregnancy. He said you weren't well brought-up. "It's all your fault," he said, blaming Mother and scolding her. He wouldn't even let her apologize. I felt sorry for her too, of course, but poor Father, being forced to say such things! It must have been hard on him.*

Sakiko wondered why Eiko would write such a thing. She had always been strangely afraid of their father. He would never resort to physical violence. But violence conveyed through words, tone of voice, gestures, and facial expressions leaves wounds that are much deeper and harder to treat than any physical wound. Hiroko said it took a special talent. Those wounds lasted forever and throbbed with pain, causing the victim grief. Everybody in the family had them, Sakiko thought, but nobody realized where they came from.

> *After that, Mother went wild; Father went off on business trips, and she took that as an excuse to take up drinking again, against the doctor's orders. She doesn't go out bar-hopping the way she used to, but at home when she gets tipsy she weeps at the memory of our grandmother and our Aunt Hanako, the one who died young. She says she can't wait for the end to come. (You know what she means by that, Sakiko? She means she wants to die.)*
>
> *So there's no way you can bring some foreigner named Paul home with you. Don't add to our troubles.*

She wouldn't go home if they paid her. After that came a letter from Fusako.

You fully deserve to be disowned, and why you haven't been is one of the seven wonders of the world. Just who do you think you are, telling our home phone number and Father's office phone number to some woman we don't know the first thing about? You can do as you damn please, but don't get us mixed up in it. Don't disgrace the family name. The effect will be felt for generations. Mother is furious, but for some unfathomable reason she seems unable to take it out on you. Instead she goes around the house drinking and muttering, "She's no daughter of mine." "I'll never let her darken my door." "I never want to lay eyes on her again." If she'd only yell those things straight at you, she and we would all feel a hell of a lot better. As it is we're slowly losing our minds.

My own personal feeling is that you should apologize by taking your life, but I guess in the final analysis that would only make her sadder. Ooh, it just makes me so mad. You never should have been born yourself and now you're going to have a baby? You've got some nerve. Abort it. If you decide to come back to Japan to do it, I'd be more than happy to make the arrangements. I'll get the money together, so hurry and let me know.

Fusako hadn't changed. This sort of thing always got her on her high horse. Sakiko smiled bitterly as she ripped the letter in two and threw it away.

She translated Eiko's letter without softening it and asked Paul what he thought.

"Looks like we'd better not go to Japan," he said, and paused before continuing with a wry smile: "My parents don't like it that you're Japanese, your parents don't like it that I'm a foreigner. It's a shame, but it looks like we've both got foolish relatives."

Whether her parents and sisters were irate because Paul was a foreigner or because she'd gotten pregnant before marrying him, Sakiko had no idea. She doubted that it was because she hadn't talked it over with them. It wasn't the custom in their family to talk things over anyway.

"If your mother is drinking and talking about wanting to die, she has a psychological problem," said Paul. "She should see a counselor."

Her mother and a counselor? Her family and a counselor, Japanese society and counselors—none of it fit together. Sakiko felt at a loss. After the war, just getting enough to eat had absorbed everyone's energy. Then life got a little easier, and two years ago there'd been the Tokyo Olympics. In four more years there would be an international exposition in Osaka. People were racing in search of material affluence. Physical health might be one thing, but for mental health, there was no room for concern.

Then when someone's behavior went so far off the rails that there was no concealing it, and they saw a psychologist or a psychiatrist, they got branded as "crazy." Her mother, always so terrified of what people would think—how could she possibly get counseling? Did the profession even exist in Japan?

From her sisters' letters, it seemed Mother had started drinking again because she'd been scolded by Father, but even if that was the direct cause, Sakiko agreed with Paul that the real issue lay deeper. When she used to live in Japan, she'd always assumed illness was purely physical in nature, but after living in the United States she'd come to realize that a person's mind could be ill, too. It wasn't a matter of becoming conspicuously batty or going out of one's mind; nobody needed to go off the rails; people living ordinary lives bore wounds or sicknesses of the heart that took a steady toll. The problem wasn't visible, and they themselves were oblivious, so not until a professional helped them to grow conscious of it did they realize anything was wrong.

Sakiko's mother and sisters had such internal problems. And lately it seemed to Sakiko that the problems were inherited anew by each generation of their family.

Back when Sakiko visited Hiroko in New York, after they'd listened to Coltrane, Hiroko had for some reason become talkative. She'd shocked Sakiko by telling a story she claimed to have heard from their mother.

When their mother, Sadako, was a little girl, she and her mother, Setsu, had lived with her paternal grandparents in the town where her father grew up, looking out on the Sea of Japan. Not long after the wedding, as soon as Setsu conceived a child, Sadako's father had set out for Tokyo alone. This was the agreement he had struck with his parents when, as only son, he'd agreed to a marriage for the purpose of providing his father with an heir.

After he found work and their first child, Sadako, was born, her father still hadn't summoned his family to Tokyo. On his occasional visits home, he would make meaningless noises about moving to Tokyo, which angered Setsu so much she would go out on the town, abandoning her maternal duties. Her in-laws let her do as she pleased, having stipulated that she was not to return to her parents' home until she had been delivered of a male heir. Sadako's care was left to the young maids.

When Sadako was four, her mother had conceived another child. Convinced that this time it would be a boy, her parents-in-law forbade Setsu from going out carousing with a force that surprised all who knew them. As a compromise, they allowed her to invite friends over to visit. At such times little Sadako was treated as a nuisance and bundled off to a relative's house. Loaded down with an assortment of gifts—things they happened to have on hand—off she'd gone with the maid leading her by the hand, down the path that ran straight alongside an earthen wall.

Her mother believed that things alone could buy people's good will; people were not nice to one another otherwise, and they didn't tell the truth. "People will say anything they've a mind to. Don't take what anyone says at face value." When they were alone, Sadako heard these words repeated constantly, as if they were the chorus to a children's song.

As she slipped off her clogs, embarrassed at her daily visits to her cousins, her aunt would greet her with a cheerful, "Everybody's waiting for you!" But one time Sadako overheard the eldest of her cousins whisper to the others, "They say Sadako's grandma used to go out carousing too, neglecting her kids, just like her mom does now." Her tone implied that Sadako's presence was annoying—so Sadako couldn't help wondering: had her aunt's greeting been a lie? Then her mother was right, you really couldn't trust what people said.

Sadako got a baby sister. The grandparents, despondent at the birth of another girl, gave her the flowery name "Hanako" to cheer themselves up.

Then suddenly her father came home. Sadako had been at the relatives' house all day again that day. When the maid fetched her and brought her home, there standing on the veranda was a tall, nervous-looking man in Western-style clothes, staring down at Hanako in the arms of one of the older maids. It was the familiar face of her father.

"So it's a girl again." He said this loud enough so that Sadako, standing off at a distance watching, could hear; he then added, "Girls are a bore." Noticing Sadako, he turned impassive eyes on her and said "You've gotten big," smiling with the lips only.

Sadako ran toward him in joy, but then, sensing that he did not want her to do that, stopped short. Her father's gaze returned briefly to the baby. Then for a while he looked out at the big pine tree in the garden, his mouth in a twist. As her father confronted the tree, which was carefully pruned in a style unique to that region, Sadako sensed hatred welling up within him. Its object she could not tell, but it came surging across the cold floorboards of the veranda in waves and penetrated her heart.

Coming back to himself, her father walked past her without a word on his way inside the house. As he went by, he mechanically laid a hand on her head. She looked up, so happy at his touch that she could have burst. But in the glimpse she caught of his face, his eyes were wandering somewhere in darkness. She touched the top of her head, attempting to transfer the feel of her father's hand to her own palm as she watched him walk off. The door closed smartly behind him.

During the few days he was there, her father was always out somewhere, or entertaining visitors, or holed up in an inner room where he took his meals alone. Sadako would creep up to the room where he was and be scolded by her mother for it, but just to have her mother at home, paying attention to her, made her happy.

She wished her father could have stayed forever, but he left. He turned the same wooden gaze on her as when he came home, said "Take care of yourself," smiling with his lips only, and was gone. Once he was gone, her mother started going out again. But Sadako wasn't alone anymore. She had Hanako. Watching the nursemaid feed her and put her to sleep, she vowed to see that her baby sister never experienced the loneliness she had known.

Her father continued living alone in Tokyo until one day, out of the blue, the family received notice of his death. Sadako was sixteen, Hanako twelve. Their father, who had been living in a rental house, left no debts, but neither did he provide anything in the way of an inheritance. Setsu decided to leave her younger daughter behind to carry on the family name and take Sadako back with her to her parents' house.

As they were packing, Hanako came by with an armload of clothes and a puzzled expression. "Why aren't we taking my things?"

"Your things will come later," Setsu said, and glared at Sadako, to keep her trembling arms from reaching out to her sister. As wicker trunks were tied with cord and loaded, and even various items of furniture packed and ready to go, Hanako wailed in a voice full of anxiety: "Are we moving?" Sadako fought down the urge to cry out to her.

On the morning of their departure, at breakfast Setsu told Hanako that they would be living apart for a little while, but that she would soon come back for her. Hanako listened wonderingly, then went to her room and returned holding in her arms a doll that had been a present from her father. She held the doll in her lap, not touching her food, eyes fixed on her mother and big sister.

Hanako followed Setsu and Sadako out to the entryway only to find her shoes missing. As she was hunting for them desperately, her grandmother came up from behind her and held her tightly in her arms.

"I'm going too! Take me!"

The sight of her sister sobbing, locked in those arms, would haunt Sadako for the rest of her life.

Sadako married at the age of nineteen. Her husband, whom she fell in love with at first sight when they were introduced by the go-between, died a few years later in a traffic accident. She was pregnant, and gave birth to a son at her in-laws' house. They treated her like a maid and wanted to get rid of her. Her late husband's older brother and his wife were childless, and unbeknownst to her they adopted her baby. Soon he stayed with them at night, while she slept in the room next to the maid. She and her son lived in different places in the same house, and he took to his grandmother and his aunt and uncle more than he did to her, his own mother. They taught him to fear her, and when he caught sight of her he would run away. Even so, she wanted to go on living under the same roof with her son.

Unwilling to see her daughter let her life go to waste, Setsu decided to have her marry again. This time her husband would be Morimoto Morimasa, a man marked for success. Sadako refused. Remarrying would mean going off and leaving her son, who had to stay put as the family heir. How could she do such a thing? Setsu had laughed away this protest. As Sadako wasted away on the meager diet her parents-in-law allowed her, Setsu insistently made the case for remarriage. Sadako's instincts told her that her mother was feigning concern, hoping to use the proposed marriage to elevate her own social status.

Then one day, Sadako was abruptly ordered out of the house. She clung to a pillar and called out her son's name, but a manservant tore her away and put her in a car. She had no idea where her son was.

She came to a decision then and there. There was no way to keep from bearing other babies. A woman had to give birth in order to live; that was all she could do. *All right*, she thought, *then I will rent out my womb. Any child I bear from now on will not be mine, it will be the man's.*

Sadako married Morimasa. It was the second marriage for them both. He had divorced his first wife for failing to give him a child. Providing an heir for Morimasa's business: this was the purpose of their marriage. She had already given birth to one son, so she was confident she could do it again. She knew perfectly well that Morimasa was attracted not just by her beauty but by her proven record (though it had been only the one time) of producing a child of the desired sex. But over the next dozen years, amid alternating hope and disappointment, the results were dismal: four girls. When she knew the last baby was again a girl, she felt so apologetic that deep down she was too ashamed and stricken to look her child in the face.

When Fusako, the third girl, was born, the National Mobilization Act had just been passed. The whole nation was excited by war; boys were needed as soldiers. This, along with her failure to provide her husband with an heir, left Sadako in despair. She thought of killing herself and the baby too. But then the sight of the two innocent older girls jumping up and down in their excitement to see their new baby sister wiped all such thoughts from her mind.

Thus ended their mother's story.

"And that," wound up Hiroko, fixing Sakiko with a look as cold and pointed as a steel blade, "is why I will never do anything so foolish as to have a baby."

2 Say No

"**D**on't you want somebody to love?"

The sound of the singer's voice could be heard all the way out in the parking lot. The baby had started kicking lately, slowing down Sakiko's movements, but at the provocative beat her pace quickened. Further in the park there was a temporary stage, and from there to the entrance where Sakiko stood next to Paul the people sitting in the crowd formed a sea of heads. Some of the heads were wrapped in colorful cloth bands, the ties draping down the forehead; others were decorated with flowers or sported one of the conical Vietnamese *non la* hats.

They wove their way through the crowd, Paul leading her by the hand, in search of a place to sit. People clearly were willing to make room for the newcomers, but they were already piled three deep, and making space was difficult.

"Let's go to the love-in," Paul had said. "It's a gathering of people who want peace, not war. It'd be good for the baby, too."

Paul, already a Vietnam War protester, had made this

suggestion once Sunday brunch was over. He hadn't needed to explain. Just the words "Let's go to the love-in"—or even just "Let's go out"—would have been enough for her to follow him. Where they were going or what sort of event it was, he didn't need to specify: even if she learned it was something she'd rather not do, she was incapable of saying no. And yet Paul had tried to tell her. Now that they had arrived and she was looking sullen, he said, "Hey, I warned you what to expect." He said this to remind her that she hadn't said no.

One person half got up and squeezed closer to his neighbor, and the next person followed suit and the next, enough people making room for them so that they could sit down. Sakiko, who was wearing an ankle-length skirt, sat down with one knee up, arms around her knee. The female vocalist in the center of the stage repeated her question: "Don't you need somebody to love?" Under a blue sky, embraced in dazzling light, the spirits of the listeners were moved, and the air echoed with their cries of response. Everyone's determination to change this country waging a useless war against a small Asian nation welled up and coalesced. Sakiko was glad she'd come.

Someone tapped her on the arm. It was the man sitting next to her. He had on a Native American-style leather vest decorated with colorful turquoise stones and beads, and a matching leather band around his waist-length brown hair, which he was wearing bound up. He had a long, neatly trimmed beard, and perfectly round glasses. Wordlessly, he held out a half-smoked joint of marijuana. She accepted it without a word and brought it to her mouth. A hand reached out from the other side and snatched it away. Paul's eyes bored into her. "Why didn't you tell him no? You're carrying our baby!"

She didn't want to smoke the joint. She knew it would harm the baby. She'd intended to say no, but the word wouldn't come out of her mouth.

"Sakiko, you're going to be a mother. From now on it's not just about you. You've got to protect the baby, too. You've got to think what the right thing to do is, and say no when you have to. You've got to say it: no, no, no."

Paul repeated the word three times as if to make sure it was embedded in her. She glanced at the man next to her, the one who had offered her the marijuana, wondering what he might think of Paul's going on like this. He was looking toward the stage, his eyes nearly shut in evident pleasure, all thought of Paul and her seemingly gone from his mind. She looked around. Everyone else was the same.

Paul went on. "Seeing the way you act, I just about lose hope. I know Japanese people care what other people think. They worry about face. But I'm telling you something extremely important. Instead of worrying what other people will think, you should be listening to me!"

As Paul's tone grew more heated, a middle-aged man sitting in front of them turned around. Sakiko bent over, trembling, her hands spread protectively around her belly, and Paul's voice said matter-of-factly over her head, "Sorry to be so noisy. I was just telling her something really important. Please understand."

The man nodded, and turned back mildly.

She understood Paul's point, but something inside drove her to act the way she did. She put her lips up to his ear and whispered the words "*gomen nasai.*" I'm sorry. Words she had known and used from childhood, they slipped out easily. He hugged her and kissed her lips, which were quivering in fear. Gently he laid his hand, the fingers still covered in dried paint, on her round belly. Hoping that someday, as a result of the steady encouragement he gave her, the time would come when she would learn to say no.

"Peace!" cried a voice from the audience, and the man next to her put his hands around his mouth and yelled back, "Peace!"

With his arm around her, Paul shouted "Peace!" in a strong voice. She shivered; for a moment it sounded as if he'd shouted "No!" She gave him a suspicious look; he pursed his lips as if to say, "It's okay," and patted her lightly on the head. Reassured, she leaned her head against his shoulder and closed her eyes.

The woman next to Paul called out in a loud voice, slowly drawing out the sound: "Peeeeeeeace." Then from all around a chorus arose, many versions of the word flitting back and forth. A flood of cries for peace, each one filled with sincerity.

Much as she wanted to, Sakiko could not bring herself to say either "No" or "Peace." Something inside prevented her.

The baby kicked. When Sakiko was inside her mother's womb, she used to kick just like that.

It was dark. Not just the room was dark; everything was. Someone wasn't glad I came into this world.

When I finally emerged from the blackness, the midwife announced, "It's a girl," her tone saying, *The baby is safely born, but unfortunately it's a girl;* and in the eyes that were turned on me in response there was disappointment and loathing. Not to be outdone, I responded by crying lustily, like an animal. If I didn't announce my own birth in no uncertain terms, my existence would be erased. All the time I was in the womb of that person who turned those eyes like firebrands on me, she had sent me a constant stream of signals: *I don't need you. I don't want you. Be aborted.*

She never spoke the words aloud or showed what she was thinking. When she found out she was pregnant, every time people said, "Congratulations! This time it will be a boy for sure," she smiled and nodded, but all the while, as I floated in amniotic fluid her heart directed a stream of arrows at me. They were without shape or substance, so no matter how many times they pierced me, I did not die. But my soul was scarred. During the months I spent in her womb, I came under constant attack, but I clung stubbornly to life and eventually was born.

Anyway, I was given a name: Sakiko.

My lullaby: "Crying kid, crying kid, they're coming to buy a crying kid." A young maid on the verge of exhaustion would scare me by almost screaming this. Then through the dim light I would hear a man's gravelly voice going by on the street: "Crying kid, crying kid." Terror made me stop crying instantly.

Back then Japan was conducting a war of invasion that it was convinced it would go on winning, and people were in high spirits. That woman's husband and my father, Morimoto Morimasa, expanded his business in the conquered territories and moved from a rental house into a large home of his own. All Japan believed the victory bulletins issued by the Imperial General Headquarters; the nation was in an excited uproar. Who would have dreamed that years after the photographer came to our house to take pictures of us four sisters in our matching kimono, a cluster of American planes would come and reduce all Tokyo to ashes? A few months later, the atom bombs were dropped on Hiroshima and Nagasaki, and Japan surrendered.

When Sakiko came out of the anesthetic, the first thing she saw was the doctor's wry smile. "And here I thought Japanese women were quiet."

Throughout her labor, she had hollered in terror, Paul informed her, holding the tip of her nose in his fingers and twitching it lightly from side to side. It had all been in Japanese, so nobody knew what she said, but one of the nurses, a second-generation Nisei, had caught a few words: *baka, kowai, gomen nasai.* Idiot. I'm afraid. I'm sorry. "What's her problem?"

the nurse had asked suspiciously. Paul had explained that those were the three phrases Sakiko often cried out in her sleep when she was having a bad dream. He was used to them. He knew to comfort her by saying "*Daijobu.*" It's all right. He turned toward campus and sang, "*Daijobu, daijobu.*" He was dancing comically, his voice overflowing with humor. The sight of him saddened Sakiko. To him Japanese words came strictly from the head, not the heart; they had no emotion. Of course to her English words were like that, too.

Paul left, and shortly afterward Ryoko came, carrying a paper bag.

"I brought what you asked for." She held up the paper bag, on which was printed "Mitsukoshi," the name of a Japanese department store. Sakiko gasped. Ryoko must have brought it all the way from Japan. It was like something that popped in from another dimension, at once intimidating and achingly familiar. Had she married and given birth following her parents' wishes, as Eiko had done, Sakiko would no doubt have been surrounded with such bags.

"All the poison in your body comes out along with the baby," Ryoko said, and Sakiko thought, *Too bad the poison in a person's heart doesn't come out, too.*

She opened the package containing a thick roll of sushi from her favorite sushi shop here in town. The vinegary smell made her mouth water, and she broke into a smile. The white woman in the next bed, wearing a pink nylon nightgown, made a face; seeing this, Ryoko called out cheerfully, "Haven't you ever had sushi? Would you like to try some?" She was so friendly and sociable that Sakiko envied her. The white woman looked back down at the paperback book she was holding, with a picture on its cover of a man who appeared to be a detective standing against the background of a night street lit by a single light. "No, thank you." After a while she summoned the nurse and glanced at the two of them happily chatting and laughing while they munched on sushi. "I can't bear to be with these uncivilized people," she said, and got herself transferred to another room, away from consumers of raw fish.

"Well, bully! With the bed next door open, you've got tons more space now." Ryoko sounded relieved, but Sakiko kept thinking of the face of her father, Morimasa, who always preached against causing trouble for others. She lost her appetite.

The nurse brought the baby, wrapped in a white blanket. Sakiko accepted the bundle thrust at her, taking it gingerly in her arms and offering her breast as instructed. The baby clamped onto her nipple and began to suckle without the least hesitation, as if to say, "This is it, this is what I need to live." As the baby tugged hard at her breast, Sakiko felt strongly that finally someone needed her. She wasn't useless anymore. She remembered how even after the pregnancy had progressed so that there was no choice except to give birth, in the frantic hope that it would be a stillbirth she had deliberately tried falling downstairs, and been chided with great gentleness by Ryoko. As she looked down at the baby and smiled, tears spilled from her eyes. Ryoko wiped them tenderly with a tissue. "What an idiot you are, crying like that."

Something cold ran through Sakiko. It was an automatic response, one deeply ingrained, to the word "idiot" that Fusako had hurled at her so many times.

Around the time the street below her window was clogging with the evening rush hour, Paul showed up bearing a big box. Seeing the baby at her breast, he whispered to it, "That's mine, you know, kiddo. I'm just lending it to you for a little while. Pretty soon I'll be wanting it back." He winked at Sakiko.

What could be in the box, with its airmail label? "Sender: Morimoto Morimasa" it said. Her father's name made Sakiko tense up. The baby in her arms was startled and momentarily let go of the nipple.

Inside the box was a set of baby clothes for *miyamairi*, the traditional Shinto shrine visit for newborns, imprinted with the family crest. Undoubtedly Miss Yamane, her father's secretary, had arranged this at his bidding. The writing on the formal *noshigami* festoon was in Miss Yamane's familiar hand, elegant and warm.

Seeing the gift, Ryoko recalled the time Sakiko's mother had declined to talk to her on the phone: "I thought she was a horrible mother then, but look, she cares about you!"

"No, she doesn't. This is from his secretary, Miss Yamane, remember? You met her..." She tried to explain, but Ryoko's face was blank and uncomprehending. The image of motherhood imprinted in her friend's mind was so radiant that it made Sakiko dizzy. Until entering junior high, Ryoko had slept nestled between her parents every night; they had fussed over her to the point of being annoying. Coming from such a home, it was no doubt hard for her to conceive of the indifference and neglect that Sakiko had endured.

Yet now, in a voice full of emotion, rare for her, Ryoko was saying, "You know, I think one reason I married a Japanese-American and came to the States to live was because I wanted to get away from my parents. Having them hover over you all the time is no picnic. There's something about motherhood, Sakiko. Something—how can I put it?—kind of negative, something dark, and you need to know that."

Now it was Sakiko's face that registered incomprehension.

A piercing ray of morning sun lit up Hideto's profile as he lay sleeping on his stomach. Paul had named the baby, after hearing from a university colleague that the character for *hidé*

meant "unique." When he occasionally saw Hideto, he would tell him, "Be unique." But this was nowhere near enough. A baby was a distraction, Paul said, and so he had taken to working at the university studio. As Paul would get ready to leave the house, Sakiko would hurl a glance at him full of resentment, as if to say "Your son will never be unique."

To her, the heavy sound of the door shutting behind him sounded like the clank of a cell door in solitary confinement. "Call me if you get lonely," he said, but the idea of phoning him at his place of work for such a trivial reason terrified her. "A man's work is sacred. The existence of women and children is rewarded as they bow down in respect and sacrifice themselves to it." Her father, Morimasa, had drummed this lesson into his family, and it continued to affect Sakiko. She wanted to ask Paul to at least come home early, but she couldn't even do that.

Ryoko had been with her every step of the way since Hideto was born, dispensing advice: "Bathe him like this, change his diaper like this." It was customary in the States to put babies to sleep face down, so you had to use a firm mattress with the crib sheet stretched so tight you could bounce a coin on it. "See? This is how tight it has to be." Ryoko had dropped a quarter from the height of her face, making it bounce, and then turned to her beaming. But Ryoko now was back in Japan, caring for her sick mother. *Why did the woman have to go and get sick just when I need Ryoko?* Sakiko grumbled to herself, resentful of someone she'd never met.

The baby at her breast tugged at her heart, too. Still, it drained not only sustenance but all her energy as well. When the baby cried for no apparent reason, anger would well up in her, and she'd feel guilty, fearful that she wasn't maternal enough, that she was a failure as a mother. To keep from looking glum around the baby, she forced herself to smile till her muscles grew stiff.

The doctor had advised her to take the baby out into the fresh air once a day, and she complied by pushing him in a stroller along the road to the beach. The stroller was something Ryoko had inherited from an acquaintance in the Japanese-American community, and that person had inherited it before that from the Beverly Hills family she worked for as a housekeeper. Its gaudy gold decorations were out of place in this neighborhood.

The fence along the side of the street was full of holes stuffed with beer cans and paper bags. Behind the fence, weeds grew like crazy. Paul and Sakiko had stopped having anything to do with the people who lived in the house beyond, which reeked of marijuana. A dozen men, women, and children lived there communally, having fixed up the decrepit house themselves. One night they had asked Paul and Sakiko to put up a couple of their friends from out of town, and Paul had said no. His reason was that the last time they did that, the people had settled in and showed no sign of leaving, and after they finally did go, some expensive tools were missing. Ever since, they'd jeered at Paul as a hack artist kowtowing to the establishment, fit only to teach college.

A near-elderly couple passed by, fixing Sakiko with a stare of undisguised racial prejudice. Probably people who had moved here from the Midwest or the East so they could spend their old age in California's warm climate.

Back when Hideto was in Sakiko's womb, Paul's parents had come from Rhode Island, out east, to see how their son was doing. They disliked the fact that his partner was a Japanese woman and had hoped that the relationship wouldn't last. Those hopes were dashed when, in front of the restaurant where they were scheduled to have dinner together, his mother,

wearing a light blue Chanel suit with white trim, reached out
a hand and pulled Sakiko's full coat open.

"I knew it!"

Paul's mother, bright-red lips twisting as if tasting something sour, groaned as she stared at Sakiko's visibly pregnant
figure. Her red-tipped fingers still clutched the edge of the coat.
Paul's father, whose stoop shoulders were draped in a dark gray
suit, averted his eyes, looking as if he had just seen something
disagreeable. His face bore so many age spots that his white
skin appeared faintly brown.

"Our grandchild will have Jap blood," muttered the mother,
but Paul, strangely calm, said only, "Let me take you guys to
your hotel," and bundled them back into the car. In a silence
devoid of intimacy, Paul drove with one hand on Sakiko's
belly beside him, as if the fetus had suffered wounds from
his parents' stares and needed soothing. The tall palm trees
lining the road on either side looked down with detachment
on the car passing below. Behind them was the afterglow of
a bright sunset.

When they arrived at the hotel, a gaudy pink building facing the Pacific Ocean, a young white doorman opened the car
door. His parents probably never stayed at hotels where they'd
have to lay eyes on help with colored skin, Sakiko thought in
a rising tide of bitterness and mortification.

"Have a nice trip back," Paul called in parting as his parents
walked off and disappeared into the hotel without a word. He
watched them go, his eyes filled with conflicting emotions,
and then said mischievously, "Did you see my father's face?
That white skin he's so proud of is changing color. At this rate,
before long he'll look just like one of those people they call
'niggers' and don't even consider human. Horrors."

"We were surrounded by the enemy, huh," Sakiko said to Hideto as she held him in her arms. She spoke in Japanese, using a four-character phrase with origins in ancient China. "Even so, your Japanese grandpa sent you a kimono for your first visit to a Shinto shrine, and your American grandma and grandpa sent you a nice card. You came into this world blessed." Listening to herself, Sakiko suddenly wondered—why did she feel compelled to tell Hideto something so utterly ordinary?

For once, Paul made it home before dinner.

"Today's your birthday, right?" he said. "I hired a babysitter. Let's go out for some sushi and then see a movie."

"Wow!" Sakiko screamed with delight and hugged him.

"Don't make such a big deal of it," he said with a wry smile.

Going out without the baby—and to a movie! Happiness bubbled up in Sakiko as she squeezed out every drop of breast milk she could and stored it in a bottle. For the first time since giving birth, she put on something she had worn before getting pregnant. It fit! The waist was a little tight, that was all. The Sakiko reflected in the mirror was not Sakiko the mother, but Sakiko the woman. She put on some makeup, smiled brightly at herself, and was ready. Now all that was left was to wait— wait for the doorbell to ring, wait for footsteps to approach, wait for a car to pull up in front of the house.

Nothing happened. She went out and had a look around. Hoping that one of the cars whizzing back and forth would turn this way, or show signs of slowing down, she kept watch with fierce intensity. The dusk grew deeper. Paul looked up from the book he was reading and spoke to Sakiko, who was lingering by the open door,

"She's late. We won't make it."

"Who did you get?"

"A student."

"Someone reliable?"

"I thought so at the time; looks like I was wrong," he said smoothly and went back to his book.

Sakiko shook violently, her lips quivered, and she burst into tears.

"This is nothing to cry about." Paul looked as if no exercise of his imagination could possibly lead him to understand. He added in a firm tone, "You're acting abnormal." This was a line he used often when he wanted to impress upon her that he had done nothing wrong.

Sakiko struck back. "You don't understand! You just have no idea what it's like being stuck in the house with a baby!"

"I know you need a break. I know it's tough being with the kid all day. But your reaction isn't normal."

Yes, there's something wrong with me. I'm going out of my mind. Sakiko stared at Paul, trying to convey these thoughts. Oh, the difficulty of trying to convey in words—English words, no less—the feelings that she had been carrying around ever since Hideto was born.

"I'm different from the other mothers."

Be like others, so people won't talk about you behind your back—people can be terribly mean. This counsel of her mother's, and her sister Eiko's, flitted through her mind. Her heart stiffened. As she shook her head violently back and forth, Paul quietly drew her close and whispered calmly in an admonishing tone:

"Different how? Tell me. No one's angry with you."

She buried her face in his chest, and while she quieted the tremors in her heart, he rubbed her back with a strong, sure hand. There was a long silence before her thoughts crept up from deep within her to emerge in words.

"When I'm with Hideto, it's—how can I say it—sometimes

it's so painful I feel like I'm going crazy. Of course I love him. So much I would give my life for him. Yet there are times when I hate him so much I wish he would just go away. The other mothers say things like that, that their kids are so noisy they wish they'd disappear, but once they say it they forget about it, like they're just letting off steam. The way I feel is different. When I'm with Hideto, something in the depths of my heart is shaken. It's as if something connected to the very root of my being is disturbed. As if I'm being negated."

A deep memory going back twenty-seven years.

Army boots tramping in the street. Air stagnant with exhaustion. The color moss green. A stench like rotten fish. Hunger woke Sakiko up. She cried; no one came. But baby Sakiko had no recourse but to go on crying. Her crotch felt muddy, unpleasant. She cried harder.

The door banged open and closed crossly. Two swollen legs beneath an old kimono with frayed hem and two skinny ones beneath an apron approached her grudgingly.

Someone picked her up. She nuzzled toward the smell of milk and began to suckle.

"Oh no! She's gone and messed herself. Phew. Come on, you gotta change her." The indistinct voice of a woman in the shadows, not looking at Sakiko as she abruptly jerked the nipple away. This wasn't a voice Sakiko recognized. The breast she was offered was constantly changing.

"No, you do it." This was a voice she knew. "My only job is to nurse her. That's the deal. You can ask the missus."

"She's out shopping again."

"Really—abandoning her own baby!"

As the woman gasped, a fleck of her spittle found Saki-ko's face below, greedily seeking the nipple again. The woman jiggled nervously, her swollen eyelids moving up and down as she checked to see how well Sakiko was nursing. Then, apparently responding to the sound of army boots tramping off, she said, "My aunt's oldest boy got his call-up papers."

"It's the same everywhere," replied the young maid. "My brother got his, too."

From then on they were busy talking about who'd been drafted. Every time the woman got excited, her nipple would jerk, breaking loose from Sakiko's mouth. Not realizing this was happening, she would urge Sakiko, "Come on, hurry up."

"That oughta do it." With that, Sakiko was handed over to the maid. The nursemaid stood up hurriedly, and the sound of her footsteps retreated. The young maid with the swarthy face laid Sakiko down roughly on the futon and stripped off the dirty diaper. Her touch was bad-tempered. Sakiko smiled at her but there was no response.

"Hooie, what a stinker! I hate babies." The words sounded heartfelt, as if she really did hate babies. She grabbed Sakiko by the legs, hoisted her bottom in the air, laid out a dry cloth and dropped her down on it with a thud. She didn't pinch her. Last time, Sakiko got pinched and let out a scream for all she was worth, and that must have scared the maid. She hurriedly did what had to be done. When she was finished, she threw a quilt over Sakiko, scooped up the dirty nappy, and scurried off toward the door, making no secret of her desire to spend as little time around Sakiko as possible. She banged the door shut and was gone. Out on the veranda, there was the sound of a bird flying off.

"It's a good thing she didn't come. How could I go off and leave my wittle baby with some student I don't even know...ooh, we had a close call, didn't we?"

Sakiko wriggled out of Paul's arms and ran over, picked Hideto up, and started cooing to him. Paul stood still, his arms now encircling empty air, and looked at her distractedly with eyes that had lost focus. Now wasn't he acting how most people would call strange?

"Want some wine? There's cheese and prosciutto too." Her heart was singing.

"Sakiko, what's going on? What's happened to you?"

She herself didn't know. Something inside had clicked.

"My wife never ceases to surprise me. I wonder what dark depths are hidden in that sweet little chest of hers? Or is it just that I don't know beans about Japanese people?" He said the words aloud, as if he were standing alone in the desert asking questions of the starry night sky.

The next moment Sakiko raised Hideto's soft little body high in the air, making him crow with laughter. A line of drool trickled from his mouth, and she caught it on her tongue.

3 "Hello, I'm Hiroko"

In the LA airport, when she saw the face of the child with clearly half-Caucasian features sitting in a stroller, Hiroko thought, *Poor little thing. That child will have a life of suffering, trapped between two races and two cultures.* Meanwhile Sakiko, dressed in shorts and sandals, was pointing Hiroko out to the child and smiling without a care in the world, as far removed as she could be from her sister's grim reflection. Hiroko responded with a smile. The same smile that made people say, *Even when you're smiling you only look sad.*

"Look, it's Auntie Hiwoko!"

The sound of Sakiko's syrupy voice gave her chills.

"Give Auntie Hiwoko a tiss."

Sakiko picked up the infant and set its sticky lips on Hiroko's cheek. Hiroko was horrified. At least no drool got on the collar of the suit she'd splurged on at a Madison Avenue boutique. If she was going to have to play along with this family charade, she'd just as soon turn right around and head back to New York.

Sakiko settled him in a child seat in the back and said, "Sit next to him, will you?" Then, in the same sugary mother-tone she said to the infant, "Auntie will sit by you. Isn't that wonderful?" Hiroko was shocked to think that motherhood could change someone so much. Well, so be it. She would observe how Sakiko had been transformed, and contemplate the nature of maternity.

She sensed the child's gaze on her and turned to face him, giving him as nice a smile as she could muster. She couldn't help it if her mouth stiffened and her facial muscles froze. It was always like this. The child looked at her as if she were odd and made undecipherable noises while banging on the edge of its seat. To think she'd have to spend nearly two weeks with this creature like a small animal! She'd been right to take a hotel room. Turning her back on the child, Hiroko looked out the window and waited to arrive at their destination.

Golden sunshine, a mixture of yellow and orange, lit up houses that looked like props on a cheap movie set. The effect was dreary. This was nowhere city, a place providing no sense of culture, no rest for body or soul. Did people here ever use their minds? For someone like Sakiko, involved only in raising a child, it was one thing, but for a person of intelligence this was no place to live. Strange that the streets were full of vehicles, with no sign of pedestrians. When she finally caught sight of some, they turned out to be blacks camped by the side of the road holding cans of beer. To her amazement Sakiko turned a corner just past them, stopped the car, turned around and announced, "We're here." Hiroko watched, stunned, as Sakiko took the baby out.

"Lucky thing the spot in front of the house was free!" said Sakiko with fervent happiness. With the child and a big carryall bag in her arms, she opened the heavy door using a number of keys. Well well, so they lived in a place with no garage.

THREE

Apparently an old shopping district had closed and been taken over by artists and hippies. The brilliant sun mercilessly lit up the ingrained dirt; it was so filthy that Hiroko hesitated to get out of the car. From the vicinity of a dumpster large enough to hold several dead bodies came a rotten smell mixed with the stench of urine. As Hiroko stood in the street holding her nose, a young white man with disheveled hair came along, dressed in old clothes, and bumped into her as he went unsteadily by. Shaking, Hiroko reluctantly clung to Sakiko, who said nonchalantly, "He's overdone it with the drugs." By "drugs" did she mean marijuana? Hiroko wanted to ask, but thought her sister might lose face, so she held back. From the way she'd spoken, it sounded like marijuana for sure. She couldn't have misheard, since they were speaking in Japanese. In which case Sakiko and Paul were living in a terrible neighborhood. Hiroko could just imagine how enraged their father, Morimasa, would be if he ever found out.

When she started to get her suitcase, Sakiko said, "You're staying in a hotel, aren't you? Then you might as well leave it here." She said it as if to say, "How funny you are."

"Leave it right here?"

"Yeah."

"I don't want it to get stolen. It's got some important drawings in it."

"Good heavens, no one's going to steal it!"

Her sister's appalled, ringing statement sounded contemptuous to Hiroko, and her temper flared.

But she was determined not to lag behind in this godforsaken place, so she left the suitcase where it was and followed closely behind Sakiko, who was carrying the child and bags. They went through the massive front door. The height of the ceiling and the spaciousness of the concrete floor—the imposing presence of the place—made Hiroko think for a moment that perhaps she too ought to rent a loft. But if she lived in a place like this, it would be crawling with people like that drug addict just now, and anyway her father would never hear of it.

Studying the works of art crowded together, she asked, "Are these his?"

"That's right." The pride in Sakiko's reply echoed off the high ceiling and walls. "There's a lot more, but Hideto's just started walking and, you know, Paul doesn't want them getting dirty, so he took most of them to his new studio. These are all just practice." Sakiko spoke with an air of triumph, every inch the professional artist's wife.

The paintings had technical merit, but lacked strength. *So this is what happens when you take a teaching job*, thought Hiroko.

Further in the house was a little space where the ceiling sloped low, ending in a sunny window. Crowded together along the wall were a rattly old refrigerator, a sink, and an oven on which the accumulated grime from long use had combined with rusted and worn-off places to form a decorative pattern of sorts. Hiroko couldn't help smiling wryly, reflecting that they all looked like something from a sculpture by Tinguely.

"These are all things Paul salvaged and brought home," Sakiko said, her pride palpable. "Even the sink is his workmanship."

So? Resisting the impulse to say it, Hiroko looked out the window and saw a space between the house and the building next door that was filled with a disorderly growth of flowering plants.

"The person who lives there has an herb garden. Smokable, if you know what I mean." Sakiko said this with a meaningful smile, and Hiroko just nodded.

At one side were some stairs made of old boards, each a

different color—more of Paul's handiwork, evidently—and when Hiroko mounted them in fear and trepidation, she found that over the kitchen in the center of a little landing was a bed. It reeked of body odor. The smell was so vivid that Hiroko turned red, and then got mad at herself for doing so. There was a crib, too, squeezed in between the far side of the bed and a railing that looked down on the space that served as Paul's studio. The idea of sleeping in a space no better than a clothes-drying platform with a roof was pathetic.

"If I'd stayed here," she asked tentatively, "where was I going to sleep?"

"Over there." Sakiko pointed absently. Following the direction of her finger, Hiroko gasped. There in the studio was a dingy sofa. That was what she meant.

"It turns into a bed." Oblivious to Hiroko's horrified, stricken face, Sakiko was waving to her child, who was near the sofa in a square enclosure covered with netting.

"We can walk to the beach from here," Sakiko boasted.

Marvelous, Hiroko responded silently, heading to the beach with her.

Years of vomit and excrement had permeated the concrete back road with deep stains and a powerful stench. Hiroko felt a wave of nausea and walked briskly forward. Pushing the stroller, Sakiko caught up with her from behind. "What's the big hurry?" she asked, surprised. Hiroko found it surprising that Sakiko was so entrenched in this neighborhood.

A seagull perched on a telephone pole stared down at Hiroko with baleful eyes. A bad living environment affected even seagulls, apparently. Her relief on reaching the sandy shore was short-lived. The relentless sun and the cold wind off the ocean clashed and fought, shaking her to the soul in terrifying fashion.

"When you live here, life is really easy. The weather is great year round, and you can go anywhere by car. People who live here never leave, they say. I'm so glad I came here and not the East Coast."

A laid-back person like you would be, wouldn't you. Once again Hiroko made a silent reply, and grinned.

"You get it, don't you!"

Mistakenly assuming that Hiroko agreed, Sakiko cried out happily. Studying her, Hiroko thought to herself that her little sister undoubtedly was dissatisfied with her life in this place. That was why she went overboard telling herself how wonderful it was, and seeking Hiroko's approval. Hiroko couldn't help wishing that it was so.

Something stunk. She went over in the direction of the smell and found Sakiko holding a dirty diaper by the edges as she washed it out in a toilet bowl. The sight gave her goose bumps. So this was what maternity could make someone do, she was thinking, aghast, when the door opened with a clatter of keys and in walked a man.

A cotton shirt of the sort of gray that someone with strong opinions about color might choose, and tight-fitting jeans. Was the effect calculated to ensure that the eyes of anyone facing him would naturally be drawn to the swelling at his fly, just below the buckle?

"I couldn't park and drove around and around till I got lucky: the space right in front of your car opened up." He came over and planted a kiss on Sakiko's cheek as she stood holding the diaper by the edges. This must be Paul. So the two of them lived like this, did they, exchanging this sort of daily conversation? That explained the poverty of his paintings, Hiroko thought.

"This is Paul, and Paul, this is Hiroko." Pointing with her chin, she introduced them, and while they shook hands Sakiko plunged both hands into the toilet and wrung out the diaper.

She'd have to eat food prepared by those same hands, Hiroko thought dizzily. Paul was making some cheerful greeting or other; his face blurred before her eyes.

What a huge distraction it was, having a child at the dinner table! When Sakiko was born Hiroko had been ten, and in between there'd been Eiko and Fusako, but she had no memory of any little children in the house. She seemed to lack any sense of family in general. During the war, when students were mobilized for labor, she'd been taken to the countryside to live near a factory and help make airplanes; that might be one reason. *Amazing that those things ever got off the ground. The ones I made must have been the first to nosedive,* she thought, and let out a little laugh. Sakiko, mistakenly assuming that the laughter was directed at her child, said with satisfaction, "He's a sweetie-pie, isn't he?" Hiroko recalled with new understanding the names Fusako used to call Sakiko: "dumbbell," "idiot."

As usual in American households, the master of the house, Paul, sought to entertain their guest; but the New York art scene he kept talking about had not welcomed her.

She was frankly jealous of the Madonna-like artists whom men fell all over. She had neither their sociability nor their maternal ability to sense what men need without being asked and lavish it on them accordingly. But once her work was recognized, it was a given that they would come to her. All she needed to do, she told herself on a daily basis, was to pour all her effort into creative work and wait for the results.

Enka, Japanese blues, started up. Sakiko found listening to the songs relaxing, grounding. They gave Hiroko the chills. The worldview they presented always reminded her of their mother and her oft-repeated words: "What will people say? You can't escape those shackles." The songs encapsulated all that Hiroko hated about Japan. She renewed her resolve never to go back. Japanese society was dominated by "what people will say" and the conflict between *giri* and *ninjo,* duty and human feelings... Japanese people were ruled by their emotions. That's why they started a war they knew they were going to lose. She thought of the vast expanse of land she'd seen from the airplane window. What had Japan been thinking, taking on this enormous country? If only they'd stopped to think, they'd have known better. That's what happened when you had a nation of people who followed the dictates of emotion rather than reason.

"Hiroko, you like *chirashizushi,* don't you?" asked Sakiko, concerned because Hiroko was pecking at her food. How rude of her, imagining that she, Hiroko, liked *chirashizushi!* She had no desire to eat any Japanese food, ever. Plain, light food like this couldn't supply you with energy. Western-style dishes, cooked with plenty of fat, were a far better source of energy. Oh, the taste of that beef stew she'd eaten after the war, when her father took her out to a restaurant! It was so rich, you just knew that people who ate such food were superior. Western things were all better. Even the food.

Taking care of the baby was tough enough, but Sakiko was apparently doing everything herself, without hiring a maid. How could she be content wasting her precious time on anything so stupid and unproductive as housework? Her lack of selfhood was appalling, and yet she seemed happy. She had chosen to surround herself with husband and child, a choice not available to Hiroko. Still, back when Sakiko had fled the prospect of an arranged marriage and left Japan to study abroad, even if she didn't have the makings of an artist, Hiroko had expected her to build some sort of a career for herself using her English. Who would have thought she could be so fulfilled just by having a family? *Well, she never did amount to very much. It looks like I'm the one who has to carry on the Morimoto legacy, after all. I'll do my best.* Hiroko wound a thin strip of egg around the tip of her chopsticks, rallying her spirits.

"After I drive Hiroko to her hotel, I'm going back to the studio, okay?" Paul said this as if it were understood, and he was just being clear.

Like the good wife that she was, Sakiko smiled brightly. "Okay."

Hiroko remembered a white female artist saying that a husband would always be forgiven as long as he said he was going to his studio. That artist had been opposed to the different expectations society had for men and women. Like Hiroko, she'd been isolated in her way of thinking. Hiroko chose to devote herself to succeeding like a man and winning her father's praise.

"Call me when you get up in the morning," said Sakiko. "Let's have breakfast here."

Hiroko responded, "I want some time to myself, so I'll call when I want you to come get me."

Sakiko's face fell. Hiroko directed a gaze toward her that plainly said, *I didn't come all this way just to babysit you and your kid; don't forget I am an artist.*

He could have let her off in front of the hotel and had the porter carry her suitcase up, but instead he said, "I'll see you to your room." That was when she knew. They rode up in the elevator without speaking, and walked down the thickly carpeted hallway. Using the key with its heavy round holder, she turned the gold doorknob and went in. Paul set her suitcase on the floor and silently put his arms around her. After that everything proceeded quite naturally. The afterimage of Sakiko's giddy happiness evoked another memory—a memory that made her respond to Paul.

✳

A dimly lit room half underground, with a single window near the ceiling. It faced a little lane, showing only the shoes of the people going by. Impossible to tell by looking if this was a hospital or a prison, Hiroko thought. Emotionally speaking, she didn't know which it was either.

"Hiroko Morimoto, 123 XX Avenue, XX Island." As she got up on the gynecological chair for her examination, the doctor, a middle-aged man holding a syringe of anesthetic in one hand, read this information aloud from a piece of paper in his other hand. Taking in her sophisticated urban air and untanned skin, he looked at her with eyes that said, *It's all a lie, isn't it, every last bit. I see right through you, young lady.*

In New York, the father of the about-to-be-aborted child in her womb had brought her two pieces of paper. The doctor held one of them, and on the other had been the hospital address. After telling her that if she said she'd come from New York they would throw her out, the man had gone off jauntily, as if to say he'd done his duty. She wished she could make him go through what she was going through now.

Fact: pregnancy, the physical result of relations between a man and a woman, affected the body of the woman alone. Some people said abortion was murder, but Hiroko believed that a woman who gave birth to an unwanted child might well end up murdering its soul. In any case she had no time to fret about such things. Steps had to be taken before it was too late. And so she had used some of her precious art supply money to buy a ticket, then boarded a plane for Puerto Rico along with a crowd of boisterous tourists. "Have a nice vacation," the taxi driver had said, and she'd given him a bright smile and gone in the hotel.

The wake-up call had roused her the next morning. Still groggy from the sleeping pill she'd taken the night before, she'd instructed the taxi driver where to go, paid the cost of the operation at the front desk, and here she was.

When Hiroko awoke from the anesthetic, a pair of dark eyes were studying her. Eyes exuding tenderness and love. A woman was gripping her hand tightly, fingernails with chipped red polish digging into the flesh. Cowering before such kindness, Hiroko averted her eyes. The woman rubbed her hand encouragingly, laced her fingers through Hiroko's and gave her hand a light shake. It felt warm. Colorful flowers embroidered on the woman's chest stirred faintly. Was this a dream? The woman began talking to her gently in a language Hiroko could not understand, probably the local patois. It sounded like she was saying "Everything's fine, don't worry." As if she had shared the same ordeal. Tears spilled down Hiroko's cheeks. At the same time her muzzy consciousness whispered, *Don't make a spectacle. Act rational.*

Several other women were in the room, lying on simple beds fitted only with dingy sheets and no covers. With brown-tinged skin and long dark hair, they were apparently locals. Surrounded by gray walls with peeling paint, the primary colors—reds and yellows—in the designs of the women's clothes created a strange gaiety amid the oppressive silence.

Ah, at last she was the same as the people whose feet she could see coming and going through the window of this semibasement room. No more nausea, no more distress over what was taking place in her womb. Hiroko felt relieved. Had she been the last? A staff person came and told everyone to go outside. Behind the hospital, the doctor who had performed their surgeries was waiting. "Do not speak of this to anyone," he said first in the local language and then, turning his impassive face slightly in Hiroko's direction, in English. His demeanor was brusque; he might have been calling the roll. All the women nodded that they understood and walked off toward the parking lot. The woman who had comforted Hiroko now gave her a hug and said cheerfully in heavily accented English, "Pick a good man." She started to walk away, turned, and winked. The bright sun of this southern island mercilessly revealed crow's feet and spots in a face without makeup. While she waited for the taxi she'd called from a pay phone, Hiroko studied the cracks in the concrete at the entrance. "Pick a good man," she said to herself with a wry smile.

The hotel was slightly removed from the noise and crowds of the beach. Its grounds were enclosed by an electric fence, and at the entrance was a guard with a gun at his waist. A five-star hotel with impeccable security. Whether or not he knew why she'd been in the hospital, the taxi driver urged her to celebrate her "cure," offering to take her to a special place only he knew about. Miffed, she wondered if she really looked like a rich woman dumb enough to fall for a line like that, while at the same time enjoying the driver's pose as a dapper man of the south and his spirits-bolstering way of talking. How liberated she felt, now that her little problem was solved.

She sallied into her room, planning to order something delicious from room service to enjoy on the tenth-floor terrace overlooking the blue ocean, when a memory crossed her mind, taking away her appetite:

I got pregnant so I married Paul. I plan to tell Eiko and Fusako, but not Father and Mother. Please understand. I'm so happy! —Sakiko.

The card from Sakiko she had found in her mailbox just as she was leaving. She'd opened it in the taxi to find a sentimental, backlit picture of young hippie-style lovers staring into each other's eyes on a mountaintop at twilight. She'd torn it in pieces and thrown it away in a trash container at the air terminal in New York. The moment she did so, she was attacked by nausea. Ran to a stall in the ladies' room. Stooped over, taking care not to soil her clothes, and spotted some dried blood on the commode. As she shuddered, her vomiting gained momentum.

In the airplane, she pondered. If their father, Morimasa, found out Sakiko had married a non-Japanese man, he would cut off her allowance; the income of this Paul or whatever his name was, an artist whose works didn't sell, would not be enough to support them; Sakiko would be abandoned by a man counting on his wife's allowance. As she imagined this unhappy scenario, Hiroko's mood brightened.

I won't say anything. I don't want to get involved in any family dispute. Especially one where I might get emotional.

Hiroko had been waiting all day. When she found out Paul would be getting in late that afternoon, she rejoiced that she would be able to paint until then, and not waste the whole day. But in the end she was unable even to read a book, let alone do anything creative. All she could do was watch the clock and periodically go to the kitchen interphone and ask the doorman, "No sign of him yet?" What an incredibly long, unproductive day.

"Your guest has arrived." The doorman's voice, tinged with excitement. She opened her door and waited for the elevator to come up, her desire to go over and wait in front of it struggling with her pride, which told her sharply that such behavior was unbecoming. She listened for the sound of the elevator stopping and drew back with a start at the sound of the doors opening.

Paul stood looking around the hall, an overnight bag in

one hand. When he saw Hiroko he screwed up his lips and cocked his head as if to say, "Well, here I am." Her pleasure was momentary; he came up and gave her a light kiss, laid his bag at her feet, and made a beeline for the phone.

"Hi, Sakiko. I just got in. How's Hideto?"

He said this cheerily, then turned to Hiroko and winked. The act of someone with a guilty conscience who was seeking to escape, she thought resentfully, and then he held out the receiver: "Sakiko wants to talk to you." Good grief.

"For breakfast Paul has café au lait, a soft-boiled egg…" She repeated the same information that had been in the letter that came after it was decided Paul would stay with Hiroko in New York. "Here's Hideto." Hiroko was forced to listen to the baby's babbling.

"Don't worry about Paul, I'll take good care of him." The statement was loaded with irony, but this naturally went over Sakiko's head.

While Hiroko made appropriate noises into the telephone, these thoughts coursed through her mind: *Paul and I are both adults and artists, operating by our own values, and we won't do anything to hurt our little Sakiko. She got jealous once just because he praised my work, which only goes to show that she has an inferior nature ruled by emotion, not reason.*

They had sex as a form of hello, after which Hiroko had intended to talk about the portfolio she would give the gallery owner Paul was going to introduce her to the day after tomorrow—but Paul went to sleep. She picked up his castoff trousers and underwear and placed them on a chair, angry at herself for doing so, and then took a shower. She used only the bare minimum in the way of skin care, toilet water and facial cream. Even so it was annoying that it took her longer to get ready for bed than a man.

The moment she got into bed, the phone rang. Not wanting

to wake Paul, she grabbed the receiver. It was Sakiko. To keep her from hearing Paul's snores, she picked up the phone body and moved off as far as the cord would reach, talking in whispers. She didn't think she was doing anything wrong; yet sitting hunched over in the cold with her hand over her mouth to muffle her voice, it certainly felt like she was doing something wrong.

"This is my wife's sister." At Paul's introduction, the portly art dealer smiled genially and held out his hand, but when Paul added, "She's a wonderful artist," his handshake went limp. He accepted the portfolio Hiroko held out the way someone on the street accepts a flyer he wasn't able to dodge in time, and started talking to Paul. For a while he held the portfolio in his hand, as if deciding how soon he could lay it down, and when they sat down around his desk he tossed it on a pile of printed matter. Still, she had to be grateful it had been in his hands at all. On her own, even with an introduction, people simply handed back her portfolio as if to say, "What business has this Asian woman got with me?"

Tossed aside and forgotten along with her portfolio, Hiroko lacked the courage to barge into the conversation. At length the two men stood up, looking cheerful, however they may have felt. She shook the man's hand again in parting and, turning her eyes to the portfolio still lying on top of the heap of paper between them, said, "I'm sure you're busy, but please do take a look." He glanced in that direction, having apparently forgotten what she was talking about, said "Yes, yes," and pushed her out into the street with a gesture as cold as it was elegant.

It would lie there forgotten until at some point someone happened to pick it up and, with or without first glancing at it, threw it in the trash. Of that she was quite certain. Tomorrow she would have to call him. When she got back to the apartment she'd ask Paul for the number, she thought, mentally inscribing this on her to-do list and marking it "urgent."

"'You're busy' I'm sure—you're Japanese down to your very bones, you know that?" Paul wrapped his arm around her shoulders and laughed. "I love that about you sisters."

A wry, deprecating smile rose up in her.

"I'm going to go around and visit some other places and then have dinner before I go back."

He patted his pocket to make sure he had the spare key she'd given him. Then he disappeared into the crowd. Though she should have been glad to be left on her own so that she could go home and get some work done, somehow she felt lonely and resentful. The din of the city had been exciting background music when she first came, making her heart beat faster to its rhythm. Now it overpowered her.

She waited for the rattle of his key in the lock. If she couldn't concentrate on her painting, might as well get some reading done, she thought, but that proved equally impossible. She switched on the TV, a housewarming gift from the head of the New York branch office of her father's company, but she had no idea how to operate it. She hunted for the manual and came across an old portfolio of hers. Back then she'd planned to make a quick splash in the New York art scene.

That was six years ago.

Today she'd hoped that by going with Paul, the one who had made the introduction, she would get some sort of reaction anyway. A rejection was better than nothing. She was tired of being ignored. Did being a woman disqualify her after all? Couldn't she be like a man?

※

When Hiroko first came into the world, the air she breathed was thick with disappointment. Having destroyed fond hopes that the firstborn would be a son, wherever she went she was conscious of stares that delivered the silent message: *If only you were a boy!* Perhaps taking pity on her, her father would say, "What's wrong with a girl? Not a thing!" In chagrin she made up her mind to be a son to him.

Fortunately the maids took care of the housework, and she didn't have to endure sewing lessons and other boring things that girls were supposed to do. Her mother never did them either, nor did she have any interest in them. Hiroko set herself to study like a boy and have people say she was too gifted to raise as a girl.

When Eiko was born, their father Morimasa had been openly disappointed at having another girl, but Eiko was an adorable child with big bright eyes, which made it all right. She could be married off to a good family. Hiroko had been a pretty little thing too, at birth, but an excess of hand-wringing about her not being a boy shaped her face into something neither masculine nor feminine but somewhere in between.

When her father gave Hiroko the compliment of telling her she was bright, she detected such apparent resignation in his voice that the corners of her eyes would prickle and her mouth twist. Seeing that, he would grow irritated and turn abruptly to Eiko, saying, "You're pretty, and sweet too." He radiated such genuine pleasure that everyone would be relieved and turn grateful eyes on Eiko, who puffed up with pride. In her heart Hiroko would cry out to her unseeing father, *Look at her, Father, see how conceited she is! Isn't it disgraceful? Why don't you scold her?*

Their mother never took any interest in either Hiroko or Eiko, but at such times she would reach out in a gesture of apparent maternal love and retie Eiko's hair ribbon. Unaccustomed to fussing with ribbons, she generally made it look worse.

Even when Hiroko shut herself up in her room and spent all

her time reading or studying, her mother never cared. *However this child grows up, it's no concern of mine,* her attitude said. And so Hiroko was always at the top of her class. Even her teachers began to say "Too bad you're not a boy," words that were sweet music to her ears.

When her mother reluctantly participated in parent-teacher conferences and was told by the teacher how splendid it would be if only Hiroko were a boy, she replied without interest, "Very well then, let's say she's a boy." The teacher repeated the story in the teacher's lounge, and it quickly spread all over the school, making Hiroko the target of many a curious stare. She didn't mind in the least. Rather than have people lament that she was the wrong gender, it would have suited Hiroko far better to be recognized as a boy.

Morimasa was giving her financial assistance, with the understanding that she would become a successful artist in New York. "How's it going? Have you planned an exhibition yet?" He phoned often, like a debt collector. Her father was waiting. She had to produce works of art. She had to find a gallery.

Where was Paul? Inside her body she sensed the semen he had deposited this morning before leaving. Her physical self had betrayed her. She was split between rational thought and emotion.

Just as Sakiko entered the bedroom, relieved that Hideto had finally dropped off to sleep, the phone rang. It was Hiroko, her voice shrill: "Paul still hasn't come back!"

"It's okay," she said. "That's typical for him."

"New York isn't like where you live! It's dangerous. What if he's in some kind of trouble?"

Thinking wonderingly that it was unlike Hiroko to worry about others like this, she started to say "He'll be fine," but before she could get the words out, Hiroko interrupted with a shriek.

"You don't know how dangerous a city this is!" Then, "You were the youngest, you were always spoiled…"

Gradually this was turning into an attack on her, Sakiko. She was used to coming under attack from Fusako, but never from Hiroko. Appalled, she held the receiver away from her ear and mouthed appropriate responses. Hideto's naptime was precious. She didn't want to spend all her energy on something so trivial. What was wrong with Hiroko, anyway?

After ranting a bit more, Hiroko regained her usual composure and dignity. "Sorry. You're his wife, and you say he's all right. I'm worrying over nothing. I do apologize." Then, before Sakiko could reply, she hung up. Sakiko stared emptily at the blocks Hideto had left on the floor. Exhausted, without so much as washing her face she crawled into bed.

In the morning when Paul called, Sakiko told him what had happened. "I couldn't arrange for her paintings to be seen the way she'd hoped, so she blew up," he said easily. "When I got back the door to her room was shut and she seemed to be asleep. I think she still is."

"I know that when you're out late or don't come home you're working, so it doesn't bother me, but people who aren't used to it would worry. From now on give her a call."

"Okay, will do," he said breezily, and the line went dead.

She dialed Ryoko's number and told her everything. "So it's probably being ignored by an art dealer that really set her off, but still, don't you think it was awful of her to attack *me?* Maybe she's jealous that I married a handsome, talented artist like Paul. In that case maybe she should give up her career and find herself a husband."

There was a short silence during which a bird hopped its way across her field of vision, and then Ryoko spoke. "If she can give it up, then she should, but I think it's better if she doesn't. My instinct tells me that if she gave up her art, something scary would happen."

Rose-tinted sunlight came through a crack in the curtains at the western window, which she had not closed tightly the night before, and Hiroko woke up. She had taken too many sleeping pills.

"Paul isn't back yet, and I'm a little worried." That was all she had meant to say when she phoned Sakiko. "It's all right": at her sister's confident reply, which sounded like a boast—*I know all about Paul*—she had lost it. Reason went out the window, leaving her at the mercy of a wave of emotion. *How could my emotions suppress my reason? How could such a thing happen to me?* Her head had flashed a warning light, but her heart had paid no heed. *So that's what psychology textbooks mean when they talk about hysteria,* Hiroko thought, beating her head, which was still feeling the effects of the sleeping medicine, with her fist.

She went out to the kitchen in her nightgown and found a note from Paul on the table saying he would be late again tonight. What could he be thinking, after she'd purposely given the maid the day off? Never mind. She should be glad she wouldn't lose any precious creative time by seeing him. *Okay, let's get going.* She looked at the clock. It was four in the afternoon.

She awoke to the touch of his lips. His voice said, "Thanks for putting me up. I'll be off now." His face looked hazy. His lips pressed against hers and she started to wrap her arms around him, but he slipped away. "I'll call you." At that she sprang out of bed, her body light, her head heavy as a stone. She clung to him from behind, behavior so unseemly that later, remembering, she could have died of shame.

"I'm having lunch with my parents," Paul said, turning to face her. Hiroko knew that one reason for this trip out East was to meet with his parents and try to repair the relationship that had grown increasingly strained since his marriage to Sakiko. But her head was dissociated from her body, which pressed against him and would not let go.

"It's not like you to be so emotional. Don't take so much medicine," he said emphatically.

Yesterday she had stayed in her studio all day, but had been unable to paint. Afraid of a repetition of the night before, she had taken a sleeping pill and gone to bed early. She never noticed when Paul came in.

Silently she pressed her body against his. Tensed for his next objective, his muscles rebuffed her, refused to melt against hers. The Hiroko of her head felt contempt for the Hiroko thus rejected.

He laid his hands on her shoulders. She used them as levers to free herself, smiling, and then he walked away. Pride prevented her from chasing after him and clinging to him, but when she heard the front door slam shut, she ran over to the window and watched furtively from behind the curtain as he raised his hand to summon a taxi. Ah, the misery.

Hiroko! Pull yourself together, her father Morimasa exhorted her.

I won't let a man like that get the better of me, Hiroko vowed, her eyes fixed on the taxi as it sped off. *I'll create works of art here that capture so much attention he'll be sorry he ever treated me like this.*

4 "What do you want me to do?"

"C'mon, let's go! C'mon."

Hideto's anxious voice weighed on her. Sakiko looked away and shook her head, unsure whether to say yes or no. She thought she heard children's voices in the distance, but it was probably her imagination. Halloween didn't start till after the sun went down and it got dark out, she'd heard.

"Mommy, please!" Hideto's voice rose in intensity.

"Shut up!"

She barked at him with a mother's fierceness, making the thin little body jump. As he peered up at her fearfully, trying to read her mood, his figure overlapped disagreeably with her own childhood self. Itching to give his wan cheek a pinch, she reached out an arm and drew it back again.

Finally the sun went down and she took Hideto, dressed up as a devil, out on the street. Ryoko had made the costume for him. After endless fittings, Hideto had been waiting in raptures for his first Halloween.

A few months before, Paul and Sakiko had moved from

their studio apartment in the artists' community to a house in a middle-class white residential neighborhood. Here, where even the smallest of the tasteful British- and Spanish-style houses had three bedrooms, the gazes cast on Hideto and Sakiko were as cold as cold could be. From beyond an invisible wall, whispers of "second-class citizen" came to her ears.

While they were house-hunting, Sakiko had followed Paul and Ryoko around in a daze, Hideto in tow. The real estate agents assumed that Paul and Ryoko were husband and wife and that Sakiko was their babysitter, and addressed Ryoko as "Mrs. Richardson," only to grow flustered when they discovered their mistake. Afterwards Ryoko mimicked their behavior and all three of them howled with laughter. Paul insisted on safety as a priority, since Sakiko and Hideto would increasingly be on their own, and after talking it over he and Ryoko had settled on this place. Once again, Sakiko's method of self-defense since early childhood had kicked in: she'd effaced herself.

Pulled by Hideto, she hurried to a street where they knew children lived. It was perfectly quiet. She'd thought children would be marching around crying "trick or treat," but she didn't see anybody. They went up to a house close by.

"Trick or treat!"

Hideto's feeble voice grated on her nerves. *Nobody will hear you that way*, she thought. Yet she herself couldn't speak up clearly in a loud voice the way Ryoko did. Her child made her mad, resembling her in all the wrong ways. She gave him a little poke in the back, and he raised his voice slightly. Now someone would be able to hear. There was a suggestion of movement in the house, but no one came to the door. She gave up and took Hideto next door. Same thing. There were two cars in the driveway and the porch light was on; couldn't they hear? After all, this was Halloween. They should be expecting kids to come calling. Sakiko's irritation grew.

On to the next house. The hall light was on, and a middle-aged blonde woman opened the door. She looked at them as if to say, "What are you people doing here at this time of night?" Her gaze rested on Sakiko with some trepidation. She seemed to be trying to recall whether she had any Asian neighbors. When she looked down at Hideto, her face broke into a smile. "The candy's all gone," she explained, handing him a dime.

At the next few houses there was no response. Hideto started to fidget and was just whining, "I don't wanna do this anymore!" when a door opened. A woman with a wrinkled face looked out, her eyes popping as she took in Sakiko's Asian features. She turned toward the back of the house and shrilly called a man's name over and over: "Come take a look, you won't believe this! Come see!" The man came running up, and the two of them took turns showering her with questions: What street did she live on and when did she move in? What did her husband do? Their words seemed edged in violence. Sakiko twitched, answering in a trembling voice and backing off a little with each successive question. The couple clearly weren't pleased, but they seemed to agree that at least she lived some distance away, so all right, let it go. Sakiko and Hideto clutched each other's hands, the tightness of their grip a painful confirmation of the fear they each felt. The wife went into the house and brought back a jar with a piece of candy stuck to the bottom. She dug this out and handed it to Hideto. Children, her gesture said, were innocent.

"Thank you." The words were scarcely out of his mouth before the door slammed shut. Hideto ripped the mask from his face. Clearly he had had enough. In a world where you had to assert yourself to get along, saddled with a mother who couldn't say no, he was starting to sense that he himself had to step up.

They trudged home. So children's Halloween took place before the sun went down. Hideto wiped away tears with his fists, still clutching his single piece of candy and single dime. Sakiko blamed herself. She should have asked Ryoko ahead of time. Self-reproach turned to anger. "Stop that crying," she told Hideto harshly, giving his back a poke. "Mommy didn't know, either."

He faltered, stood still, and looked up timidly at her, a strained smile on his face, as if to say, *See, I'm not crying. Don't be mad, Mommy.*

Hideto woke up crying in the night. He'd done it the night before, too. Startled awake by his screams, Sakiko got up and in desperation hauled him off to the bathroom. She shivered in the chill air. Supporting himself on the edge of the toilet, Hideto stared with frightened eyes at his mother as she shut the door and left him there. Sakiko was frightened too.

With her arms clasped around her knees, she sat in the cold, hard hallway, put her face up close to the bathroom door, and listened for sounds from within. He had long since given up on asking for help, but she could hear muffled sobs rising up uncontrollably. Tears fell on her shaking knees. Tears that missed formed a small pool on the floor.

The crying stopped. It felt to her like an unbelievably long time had gone by.

She opened the door. Hideto squirmed and tried to get away, but she grabbed him hard by the hand and led him back to bed. "If you cry, you'll get scared again," she said with a cheery smile, covering him with a blanket and giving him a kiss on the cheek. His brown eyes looked up at her in confusion, unsure if Mommy was scary or nice.

When she happened to mention Hideto's bouts of crying in

the night, a Japanese friend had advised her to sleep with her child. She took it up with the doctor.

"It will get to be a habit, so you shouldn't do it." There was contempt for the customs of an inferior culture in his voice and condescension in his eyes. Sakiko obeyed the words of the white male doctor.

Paul was staying over at his studio again that night.

The nursery school enclosed by walls of pale pink. Hibiscus flowers in bloom. A line of colorful station wagons and sedans belonging to the other mothers who had come to pick up their children. Sakiko looked on enviously at the women heading carpools, whooping children piling happily into cars. She edged her car forward to the entrance. When the teacher standing by the door saw it was her, she smiled, turned around, and called Hideto's name. Slowly he emerged, and the teacher spoke calmly to him as she opened the rear door and got him settled. The sound of the rear door shutting was Sakiko's cue to move slowly ahead.

From the back seat Hideto asked with an air of casualness, "Can I ask Daisy to come over and play?"

Every day he asked the same question, and every day it gave her a start. She bit her lip and stared straight ahead. What should she say to him? Who was Daisy, anyway? Even if she had known, she could never have gone up to that child's mother and spoken to her. She didn't have the courage. And yet if anybody had asked her what she wanted most of all right now, she would have answered unhesitatingly, "A friend for Hideto." Thinking this, an image of the carpool, its members chatting amiably, rose in her mind and dazzled her. Discouraged by his mother's silence, or perhaps accustomed to it, Hideto was looking out of the window with a vacant expression.

When they went into the bathroom and she helped him pull down his pants, her face on a level with his, the same question burst out. "Can I ask Daisy to come over and play?"

Worn down by the strength of his determination, Sakiko nodded, but she felt it was hopeless.

Again, as soon as she heard the teacher close the door, she took that as her cue to start the car forward, moving slowly so that she could stop at any time.

"That's Daisy's mommy's car!" The excitement in Hideto's voice took her by surprise, and she hit the brakes. Hideto had his face pressed to the window, and parked just ahead of him in his line of sight was a bright red Mercedes Benz with the top down. "Look! Daisy's getting in!"

A little girl with blonde hair tied up in pink ribbons bounced into the back seat. Orange and yellow sunlight played on a full-cheeked face that was smiling fit to burst. The woman in the driver's seat, wearing fashionable sunglasses etched with a delicate gold design, was leaning out to chat with the teacher. Other mothers paused that way to say hello to the teacher and pass the time of day. Sakiko, mindful of her father Morimasa's admonition never to keep the people behind you waiting, couldn't do it.

"Daisy's mommy has a red car."

Hideto was murmuring this to the yellow Bert on his Sesame Street lunchbox. Sensing in his murmur the plaintiveness of a child whose mother didn't belong to the mothers' group, Sakiko cursed her inept social skills.

Several days later, after Hideto got in the car, she stopped the car on a side street and waited for the red Mercedes Benz. Clasping hands that had started to shake from nervousness and unease, she slid them under the steering wheel. The children must have talked it over, for when Daisy spotted Hideto she said something urgent to her mother and the Mercedes Benz, the top down again today, pulled over. A pair of blue eyes looked at her, eyes shadowed by blonde hair that spilled against tanned skin—skin that clearly received leisurely, thorough care after drinking in the sun. An emerald-studded pendant swayed on her bosom, the neck of her white blouse unbuttoned just low enough to suggest cleavage. Daisy, her face thrust up beside her mother from behind, smiled at Hideto and waved. Spurred by the gesture, Sakiko forced words out of her mouth.

"I'm Hideto's mother. I wondered if sometime Daisy couldn't come over to our house after school to play."

"I've heard about it from Daisy. I'm sure the children would be delighted," the mother replied with a smile that was charming yet artificial.

The children might be delighted but it would be a pain for me: that was the message Sakiko picked up from her smooth way of talking. How to answer? The more she struggled, the more impossible it became for her to get out any words at all. As the other car moved off, fragments of words floated back, something that sounded like "I'll talk it over with my husband." Hideto fell back against the seat as if struck by disappointment.

There was no answer from the other mother, and Hideto's "Daisy's mother has a red car" and "Can I ask Daisy to come over and play?" were spoken half in tears, mingled with resignation and a touch of self-pity. Finally, Sakiko told Ryoko the whole story. Ryoko roared with laughter. Not long afterward, she went to pick up Hideto in Sakiko's place, first confirming "A red Mercedes, right?" and ultimately settling a play date with Daisy.

"I owe you!" Sakiko hugged her, and Ryoko said over her shoulder, "She said she'd pick up both of them at nursery school and bring them here."

Anxiety came over Sakiko as it sank in that the other mother would be coming over too. Sensing this, Ryoko reassured her, "Any mother would want to check out the place she's sending her daughter to play. "Besides," she added lightly with a grin, "we're yellow monkeys, don't you know."

Yellow monkeys, bananas…the epithets thrown at Japanese Americans were always on Ryoko's lips. That was a sure sign that she'd been wounded by them at some point, according to Paul, but in that case why not just lock them up in her heart, Sakiko wondered.

Casting anxious eyes at Hideto's excited romping, Sakiko began to debate whether or not to have Ryoko come over on the play date.

"Ryoko would be glad to come," said Paul, eating his dinner in haste. The restless way he plied his knife and fork conveyed the message, *Can it, Sakiko.*

Hideto looked at her with a question in his eyes: *Why isn't my mommy like the other mommies?*

"She'd be glad to come," Paul repeated, swallowing the last bit of his pork chop, and then kissed Sakiko and Hideto, grabbed his keys, and flew out the door. Hideto, apparently having decided to be on his best behavior since Daisy was coming over, ate everything on his plate and even helped clear the table.

As she did the dishes, the touch of the water brought back long-forgotten memories of Sakiko's second self, the imaginary Yuko. Since entering college, she had stopped dreaming of her. When she had gotten to know Paul, he had marveled that there seemed to be two Sakikos, but at some point he'd stopped saying it.

"Mommy!"

Had he been calling? The irritation in Hideto's voice pierced her heart.

"It's from Daisy's mommy!"

She looked at Hideto's flushed face and shining eyes. He clutched the receiver as if there were something precious on the other end of the line, and her body began to tremble.

There was the sound of a television in the background. Sounding a little on edge at calling someone unfamiliar, the woman confirmed that they were coming over the next day. Without time to think, Sakiko said, "I'll be expecting you," then immediately regretted it. "I'll be looking forward to it" would have been better. Beside her, shrinking into himself like a small animal torn from its mother, Hideto looked up at her.

Though her speech had been flowing and elegant, the woman ended the call by hanging up with a bang. Still holding the receiver to her ear, Sakiko dialed Ryoko's number with her left index finger. She was rushing, on top of which her finger was shaking, so she was unable to dial properly and had to do it over several times; the idea of switching the receiver to her other ear and dialing with her right hand never occurred to her.

When Ryoko realized that Sakiko wanted her to come over, she declared, "Seriously? I can't believe it. You'll be fine by yourself. For God's sake, be a little independent."

The red car drove up and stopped right in front of Sakiko and Hideto. Hideto hopped up and down. Daisy, whose hair was done up in colorful ribbons, started to open the car door. Her mother restrained her, got out and looked around slowly, and seemed to satisfy herself that the neighborhood was up to her standards before opening Daisy's door. Sakiko said a nervous hello and invited her into the house. The mother was wearing a low-necked white linen dress with a design of flowers blooming in profusion, and she had on the same emerald-studded pendant she'd worn the other day.

"I can't stay," she said, thrusting out lips thickly coated with red lipstick the same shade as her car. Unable to conceal her eagerness to check out how they lived, she walked briskly up the stepping-stones through the front lawn. As Sakiko's eyes took in her sandals, sparkling with gold and transparent stones, she recalled that Paul had forgotten to mow the lawn even though she had specifically asked him to.

Once inside the front door, the mother stopped and looked all around as if inspecting the interior. She paused at Paul's paintings and asked whose they were.

"My husband did them."

"Oh really. So he's a painter." She sounded disdainful.

Sakiko managed to say, "He's a professor at UCLA," and felt proud of herself for having the wits to do so.

"Oh really," the mother said again. This time she sounded approving. Her expression said that in that case, this was a place where she could reasonably let her daughter play.

"Would you like coffee or tea?" Sakiko asked.

"I'm in a hurry, so neither," came the rushed reply, and then, as if she had just remembered something of great importance, the mother continued, "Oh yes! I used to have a Japanese housekeeper. You look just like her. She was a good worker, and never stole anything. Let me see, what was her name? Riko, that's it. There just aren't any housekeepers like that anymore. You wouldn't happen to know anybody, would you?"

Sakiko was used to this sort of request. Ryoko always got incensed, complaining it was no way to treat Japanese people, but Sakiko didn't mind. Or maybe it was just that other things weighed on her so much more that she didn't have energy to spare on this.

The mother went to Hideto's room, where the children were playing, and told her daughter she would be back to pick her up after doing some shopping. "You love shopping, Mommy," cried Daisy, "so take a looong time!"

"I'll take Daisy home." The words stuck in Sakiko's throat, and as she was trying to get them out, the mother laid the basket she was carrying on top of the Korean chest in the vestibule. "Give her what's in here for a snack. Don't give her anything else, please. I'll see you later, then." She looked steadily at Sakiko as she spoke. Her gaze was so overbearing that Sakiko's "I'll take Daisy home" vanished without a trace.

As the mother opened her car door, red fingernails flashing, she turned and called emphatically, "Don't give her anything else. All right?" Her high-pitched voice rang out, and Sakiko worried what the neighbors might think.

Sakiko saw Eiko, her hair in braids, seated among the parents. She was tense, wearing her junior high uniform, and her wide-open eyes declared how alone she felt. She was used to caring for her two younger sisters, but attending the entrance ceremony for elementary school made her nervous.

Sakiko was quite used to having her sister stand in for their mother. Having her mother show up would have been more disturbing. This was just after the war, when society was still at loose ends, and no one paid the slightest attention to a girl taking on the role of parent.

After the ceremony, the parents began to exchange greetings. Eiko surveyed the scene and gradually edged back. Squeezed out of the crowd, she stood isolated, looking on sorrowfully at the first-graders with their teachers. Her expression grew more and more pained, and when the parents began gravitating toward their children's teachers to say hello, her face crumpled and her eyes filled with tears. Sakiko, who had been following her sister's movements, ran over and begged, "Take me to the bathroom!" At home when she had to pee she took off her underpants. What would she do now, wearing shoes? Apprehension got the better of her, and she burst into tears. Eiko's cheeks were wet, too, as she struggled to help her sister get her things off.

When they came out of the lavatory, Eiko set off, pulling Sakiko by the hand with an iron grip. They went out the school gate, slowing their pace when the school was no longer in sight, and finally slumping home.

"You ninnies!" The moment they came in the house, Fusako's sharp voice rang out. She stood planted before the fusuma sliding door with arms akimbo, glaring at them with spite-filled eyes. She had been watching from the window, and at the realization that neighbors would have seen how undignified—how very un-Morimoto—her sisters looked, her pride rebelled. Eiko ignored her and climbed the stairs to her room on the second floor, her steps firm as she went.

After making sure Eiko had gone into her room, Fusako stood several steps up on the staircase and imitated their father Morimasa's preachy tone: "You break down and cry at the slightest little thing. That's the trouble with women and children. Coming home in tears from a school entrance ceremony—where's your Japanese spirit? From now on you've got to do your best in school to help rebuild this country. This is no time to be crying."

After hearing Sakiko explain her fears, Fusako declared, "You brainless nincompoop! You abandoned kid found under a bridge, who was your mother, a beggar? A whore? An idiot?" Then, parodying a popular song of the day, she sang,

Kuroi ringo ni kodomo ga dekite
Damatte mite iru aoi sora.
Kodomo wa nanimo iwanai keredo,
Kodomo no atama wa karappo da
Kodomo kawaiso, awareya kodomo

96

A black apple conceives a child
And the blue sky watches in silence.
The child says nothing,
But the child's head is empty.
The child is pitiful, a pathetic child.

Sakiko covered her ears and went to hide in the parlor closet, praying that Eiko would quickly regain her spirits and come make Fusako stop.

There was the sound of the parlor door sliding open, and Eiko's assured voice: "Fusako, cut it out."

The singing abruptly stopped. To Sakiko's disappointment, Eiko did not give Fusako a scolding, but swiftly opened the closet door.

"Sakiko, you'll get lice on the bedding. Come on out of there."

Her tone was harsher than when she had addressed Fusako. She seemed worried that Sakiko might have picked up lice at the entrance ceremony, *but why oh why does she have to talk this way to me,* wondered Sakiko. Fusako was the bad one.

When Sakiko came crawling out, Eiko marched her to the bathtub, stripped her naked, and scattered white DDT powder on her head. She rubbed it into the scalp and then used a battered washbasin to scoop up cold bathwater left over from the day before and give her head a dousing.

"It's too cold!" she wailed.

"Quit complaining all the time," said Eiko, and splashed more water on her head. Behind her Sakiko could hear Fusako's disdainful laughter.

That night, Sakiko developed a fever.

"She has a cold," said the doctor who came to examine her. "If she stays in bed and takes her medicine, she'll be fine." Eiko was in a dither, afraid this was her fault. The doctor looked at her sympathetically, as if to say, *You have it tough, don't you, having to be the mother,* and then he left.

Fusako, out of sorts at having been given an order by Eiko, came upstairs with a bowl of cold water and a cloth. She used one foot to slam the door shut, shaking the rattly old house that had survived the fires of war, and spilling water on the tatami. After wiping it up she soaked the cloth again and laid it on Sakiko's forehead. The water dripped down, wetting Sakiko's hair and pillow, but Fusako only giggled.

"Everybody's busy, so don't call anyone." The door slammed shut again, and Fusako went clattering downstairs. She had turned off the light, so the only light in the room came from the hallway, filtering through holes in the torn paper door. Though Sakiko was used to this, she still felt forlorn.

What time did her mother come home that night? She waited drowsily, but her mother never came to look in on her. Her father, Morimasa, who staked his all on his business, spent the night out somewhere.

Hideto was asleep. Sakiko was enjoying the local Japanese paper while drinking plum wine and munching on rice crackers. She felt like taking a little break from the doggedness of American society.

The phone rang. At this hour, nearly midnight, it could only be Hiroko.

Hiroko's foggy voice rasped in her ear. "Can't sleep." That was how she always started off. Whether from alcohol or sleeping pills, her speech was slurred. Despite the state her sister was in, after a day with Hideto Sakiko was glad of the chance to talk with another adult, and in Japanese.

"I've been thinking of getting a driver's license," said Hiroko. "Surrounded by buildings like I am, sometimes I get this unbearable longing for nature. I could go for drives in the country."

Imagine that, Hiroko driving—Hiroko, who before hitting the accelerator or the brake would undoubtedly pause to ask herself why she was taking that action. Pitying the unsuspecting drivers of New York, Sakiko murmured politely, "Good idea." At the same time she snapped her fingers on the head of a stuffed Big Bird doll. Before Hiroko could go on, Sakiko blurted out her litany of complaints. How she had spent her day taking Hideto to and from nursery school, doing some housework in the interim, getting in a little reading. How boring it was to live the life of a stay-at-home housewife and mom. Not long ago Hiroko would have rejected such a topic flatly—"Rubbish!"—but today she listened in silence.

"What about Paul?"

Here it comes! Sakiko answered slowly, "He's not here, of course."

"Where'd he go?"

Another familiar question. Obviously she wasn't asking out of concern for Sakiko. At her end of the line, Hiroko seemed to be squirming restlessly.

"His studio. He's getting ready for an exhibition, so he's got his hands full." Sakiko offered this stopgap answer.

"Why doesn't he put a phone in the studio?"

"He doesn't want to be bothered."

So far, this was the same as always. But then Hiroko said something unexpected: "That would be a problem in an emergency." The statement struck Sakiko as out of character, since her sister wasn't the type either to imagine emergencies or, if one did arise, to care much. She wondered about the remark.

"If anything happens, there's always Ryoko."

"Oh, her. That simpleton."

"You say that about everyone," Sakiko protested. There was no response.

After a pause, Hiroko said, "You're great, Sakiko. It never occurs to you to have any doubts." Her tone was bantering.

"Doubts about Ryoko? How so?" Sakiko felt as if she'd taken a punch in the gut.

The line was quiet. In the background a car horn sounded, echoing in the valley between buildings.

"Who said anything about Ryoko?"

Sakiko was taken aback. "You just told me to be suspicious of her." Her words were swallowed halfway to New York.

Silence again. Sakiko turned to Big Bird and made a face.

Hiroko spoke, sounding as if her emotions were catching in her throat. "You think Paul works in his studio every night."

Sakiko was thunderstruck. What was Hiroko getting at?

"Speaking as a fellow artist, it seems to me his going to the studio is just an excuse. To be exact…I'd say he's involved with someone."

Her last words came out the way someone forced to attend a family dinner might say in English, "Please pass the salt." Reeling at the gap between what her sister said and how she'd said it, Sakiko grabbed Big Bird and beat her head with the toy in an effort to recover her senses. The newspaper at her hand rustled.

"What was that?" snapped Hiroko, her nerves unusually sharp.

The strange sound went through Sakiko's ears and froze her, rendering her capable of saying only "Newspaper. Arm. Touched it." She thought she heard Hiroko exhaling, and then the line went dead.

With too many passengers aboard, the bus came wheezing and gasping to the stop, lingered a moment, and lumbered away. When it was gone, there stood her mother. She was wearing old-fashioned work pants, and on her head was a scrunched-up towel in danger of slipping off. Her knapsack, which hadn't held food when they left home, now seemed heavy, as if it contained potatoes. She seemed to want to rest a little before she started walking. If she hadn't seen little Fusako and Sakiko across the way, she probably would have crumpled to the ground. The girls flew to their mother's side and walked beside her, tugging on her hands. She let them do as they liked, saying nothing and showing no emotion. Sakiko, who'd never had any opportunity to be around her mother like this before, was so thrilled she wanted to stay where they were forever.

Early one morning after the air raids in Tokyo had grown fierce, Sakiko left home with her mother, Eiko, and Fusako, carrying a knapsack filled to bursting. They got on and off crowded electric-powered trains and steam locomotives, and many things happened that she didn't understand, but she never eased her grip on Eiko's hand and eventually they got off a bus someplace surrounded by green fields.

They began to live in a little house at the edge of the fields. At dawn every morning, Eiko and Fusako lined up with the other pupils and set off for the school, a good distance away. Fusako would be sobbing in pain at boils caused by malnutrition as Eiko dragged her off. After that, their mother would pack her knapsack with kimonos to exchange for food and go off on the bus, leaving Sakiko to fend for herself until her sisters came home. The local children called her an "evacuated kid" and wouldn't play with her, so she watched them from a distance.

One day, an older boy Sakiko hadn't seen around before came up to her and said, "I'll play with you. Come with me." Apparently out of school with an injury, he dragged one leg that was wrapped in a dirty bandage. Seeing her fear, he held out a steamed sweet potato. "I'll give you this, so come on."

She reached out, and as the sweet potato moved back slightly she took a step forward to grab it. The sweet potato moved again, and she followed it. In that fashion, they went into the woods.

As she finally got hold of the sweet potato and bit into it, she realized that she was surrounded by children. None of them were girls, which struck her as strange, but she was more drawn by the wonderful feel of the sweet potato in her mouth. She swallowed the last of it and turned to go home. Gleaming eyes surrounded her like barbed wire, trapping her. The oldest boy grabbed her by the shoulder. She made no attempt to resist. She just didn't know enough to protect herself.

The oldest boy laid Sakiko on the ground and ripped off her underpants, saying things like "sickness" and "doctor" in a shrill and nervous voice. The other boys gathered around and stared at her, holding their breath. Then they fought with each other to play with her between her legs. She didn't know what was happening, but the atmosphere of stagnant excitement made her feel that it was all somehow shameful, and it hurt.

"Scram!" At this word from the oldest boy, they all fled. Her skirt was up, her fanny exposed. She put some spit on the place that stung. There was blood on her finger. If it never stopped bleeding, what would she do? What if it hurt even more? But apparently she wasn't allowed to tell anyone what had just happened. She'd heard the oldest boy telling the younger ones threateningly, "Keep your mouth shut," and "This is a secret, okay?"

If people at home knew about this they would get mad for sure, and scold her more than usual. Mother would turn her eyes from her as if she were a piece of filth, and ignore her. "You mustn't tell anyone," Eiko would say. "If you do, we won't be able to stay here, and we'll have to go back to Tokyo where all the bombs are falling." She would look all worried and upset, as if this were really going to happen. Fusako would be delighted, and tease her about it with a vengeance. Sakiko felt such anguish she could scarcely breathe. She looked around for help, but the trees in the setting sun only turned cold eyes on her.

"Where'd you go?" Eiko called, never lifting her eyes from the book at the table where she sat studying. Sakiko glanced inside the house and then lingered in the doorway with downcast eyes before entering timidly. She took a pair of underpants from the box in the closet that served as chest of drawers and went to the toilet to change. This toilet wasn't the kind that flushed, like in the Tokyo house, so as she took off the old panties and put on clean ones she had to struggle not to fall into the deep pit where shit dropped with an eerie sound. It was hard going, and she felt like crying.

She had a secret, so she couldn't take off her pants in the hallway like always. Not knowing why she had to keep it a secret made her more nervous. She'd only get scolded for using the water in the kitchen, so she washed out her pants with well water that she dipped up after knocking the bucket over several times.

At some point Fusako had come and was standing, watching. "Five years old and you wet your pants." Even muffled, her voice dripped with scorn. Sakiko glanced fearfully up at Fusako; behind her stretched the fields where dusk was falling. The place between her legs stung, and she looked back down at her pants, scrubbing them hard.

When their mother came home, she looked at Eiko and had her remove the knapsack. "You do the rest," she said, and lay down to sleep on the spread-out futon. The sisters sat down for supper at the low table, gathered around the aluminum potful of soup with flour dumplings that Eiko had made. They ate quietly to keep from waking their tired mother, but Eiko and Fusako bickered as usual: "How many pieces did you eat?" "No fair!" "Pig." Sakiko held back because she was the youngest, but she wanted more just as much as they did. She said nothing for fear of being yelled at.

Sometime later Sakiko was awakened by a loud disturbance. For a while there was the sound of her mother and Eiko quarreling, and then they sprang up and began to scuffle. Her mother pinned Eiko down on the futon, straddled her and wrenched her arms up. Eiko screamed. Her mother shrieked, "I'll kill any child of mine who defies me!" The two figures were lit by moonlight streaming in through cracks in the shutters, and then her father's figure joined them, doubling Sakiko's terror.

Since coming here their mother had grown hot-tempered, especially after she started shouldering her knapsack and setting off to buy provisions. Poor Eiko bore the brunt of her anger. What if she really got killed? Then Mother herself would suffer since she wouldn't have anyone to do cooking and cleaning in the maid's place, thought Sakiko, wiping her tears with the thin towel Eiko had laid over the quilt.

Fusako lay trembling in her futon beside Sakiko as their mother pulled Eiko up by the arms, now tied behind her with a sash, and kicked her in the back. Eiko wept and repeatedly moaned, "I'm sorry," but the apology did not register on their mother in her frenzy.

Their sister Eiko might really die. No, Sakiko told herself, she wouldn't, since the same thing had happened before and she didn't die then. Sakiko had witnessed such scenes many times over; she could never forget them, however she might try.

Paul was drinking wine, Sakiko green tea. It was Sunday, and for once he hadn't gone out. They'd taken Hideto to the beach, getting him so tired out that afterwards he took a long nap, ate some supper, and went right back to sleep. A perfect chance. Now they could talk quietly. She avoided wine to keep herself from getting emotional. Her physical condition was fine. Time for a cool-headed talk. She took a deep breath.

Paul's eyes were on the lingering sunset glow behind the redwoods. Looking at him, she sensed it would be better not to speak, but her lips moved of their own accord.

"You know something, Paul," she began calmly. He looked at her in mild surprise. *Stay calm,* she told herself, and continued. "My sister Hiroko calls here every night…and she sounds funny." Another deep breath.

"Funny? How so?" His blue eyes looked at her tenderly, the surprise gone. Even so, Sakiko felt tense, and went on nervously.

"I don't know. It's hard to explain. There's just something funny about her."

"Probably her art isn't going well." Paul looked back at the light in the sky. He sounded curt.

Sakiko murmured in Japanese, "There you go, avoiding the issue."

Her heart felt a chill, and there was a tickle in her throat. She tried to talk and went into a fit of coughing. She took a drink of tea, sat up straight, and stole a look at Paul. She could see through the mesh of his gray sweater that a red warning light had gone on: *Mustn't do anything to excite Sakiko.* Right. Sakiko might explode at any moment.

She drank her tea noisily and, just as she'd planned, Paul looked at her. His eyes were searching. Sakiko slowly took another breath and planned her next words. Without yelling. His eyes were glued to her, watching suspiciously. She couldn't find the words she wanted, which annoyed her and sapped her confidence. Her feelings shifted to fear. She was afraid she lacked the ability to verbalize what she wanted to say, and she hated herself for it.

"I won't get angry, so go ahead and say it." Paul's tone was cool and businesslike.

"Hiroko…"

Paul's face twitched, and the wineglass in his hand shook slightly. This was evidently a topic better avoided. He didn't like talking about her sister. No doubt when he was in New York Hiroko had harped about her work not being recognized, and he'd had a bellyful. Even so she repeated the name "Hiroko," trembling bit by bit.

"What about Hiroko?" He was really saying *Never mind her, what about you?* Reassured by the evident concern in his voice, Sakiko went on.

"She's acting funny. She calls every night, and she sounds strange," she said again.

"Hiroko definitely has issues. Her ambition is over the top. In a sense I think she's emotionally ill." Paul said this dispassionately, in the tone of a professor covering the content of a textbook he had used for years, before adding, "Sakiko, you can't do anything for her. She won't listen to advice or admonitions. The only thing that can save her is her art."

At the word "art" Sakiko's hand automatically reached out, and her fingertips picked up a slice of sashimi and put it in her mouth. There was no soy sauce on it, but it had no flavor anyway. Spoken by Paul, the word "art" always had a magical effect on her. That one word meant all was accepted, all forgiven.

Sakiko fell silent. Her emotions were running high, and she didn't trust herself to open her mouth. "Keep calm," she whispered to herself again, and reached for another slice of sashimi.

Paul went on, still in professorial mode. "You sisters have lived dominated by your father's shadow. Absolutely dominated. Hiroko longs for his praise and admiration, and you're terrified of him. Hiroko has made it her life's goal to debut in the New York art world so she can earn his praise. It's unhealthy. And it's not working out the way she wants it to, either, which is why she phones you."

Sakiko nodded, but doubt soon sprang up. Was it really only that? "But…" She started to speak, but Paul closed her mouth with a piercing gaze.

I'd say he's involved with someone. Hiroko's words lay heavily on her heart. That comment had nothing to do with Hiroko's art. She'd said the words with such suppressed emotion that they lingered strangely in the air.

Sakiko hesitated, then blurted, "I want you to put a phone in the studio. I worry. What if something were to happen? As long as only I know the number and we don't tell anyone else, it wouldn't be any bother to you." Her voice shook, tapered off. Her upper body was bathed in sweat.

Beyond the now-dark trees a car went by, its headlights raised. The elderly white couple living at the end of the street were just back from the beach club. The two of them spoke often to Paul but not to her. They only said hello and turned away. Still, that was better than the ones who talked to her as an act of charity toward a member of what they saw as an inferior race. Behind their kind demeanor lurked feelings of superiority that now and then came to the fore: as long as she agreed with what they said (usually didactic) all was well, but when they realized that she differed from them even slightly their attitude was, "You have no right to your own opinion."

Paul got up, came over with his arms spread out, and embraced her. His muscles conveyed the message, *What's wrong?* His hands slipped under her wet T-shirt and gently caressed her breasts before moving lower, inside her shorts. She was surprised to find herself letting him know with every part of her body that she was not about to be carried off to bed just now.

His fingers stopped moving and he touched his forehead to

hers. Lightly he said, "Sakiko, I can't put a phone in the studio."

"Why not?" she started to ask, but her pursed lips trembled, and she couldn't speak. He went on.

"People who come and go there would know I had a phone. I'd have to tell them the number. Once I told one person, I couldn't very well keep it from the others."

"You don't care what happens to Hideto and me?"

"There's always Ryoko."

Ryoko again. You leave me and Hideto to her, and go your merry way. You should never have had a family! she shrieked silently.

Suddenly, like a gush of water, a scream escaped from her mouth: a flood of words without meaning, beyond her control. Paul's gaze reverted to the darkness outside, as if to say, *Here we go.* Engulfed by the sense that she was being ignored, she cried out in tears:

"Art, always art! Your friends look down on me because I don't do anything creative. So does Hiroko, and so do you. I want to do something, too."

She raised the hem of her T-shirt to wipe her eyes, uncovering braless breasts. Paul's hand immediately reached out and she swatted it away, saying automatically, "Who's going to watch Hideto?" The same old phrase.

"Sorry," he said. "I shouldn't have done that. Let's talk this out calmly."

His maddening placidity drove her to pick up her teacup and hurl it at his painting on the wall. Voiceless words were wrung from her: *Stop fooling around, take me seriously!* The cup broke, leaving only a smudge on the protective glass. Superimposed on the smudge she saw Fusako's face, a disagreeable smile playing about the lips: *The way you act is so immature!* Sakiko reached for the wine bottle.

"Throw it! Smash the damn thing. Go on, do it!"

Realizing he meant it, she cooled down and her strength ebbed. Her anxiety and dread vanished. She let go of the bottle and stood there like a mute squirrel. He grabbed her hand and pulled her into his arms.

"I…love…you," he said with force, in a voice that seemed to rise out of the earth.

I don't ask for love, Sakiko thought. *Just don't ignore me.*

"Your father will be home for dinner."

Mother's voice was trembling with nervousness. Eiko and Fusako went stiff with fear. Sakiko, just ten, felt her eyes mist over with dread. The mere thought of her father, Morimasa, sitting imposingly at the dinner table took away her appetite. She envied her sister Hiroko, who ever since becoming a college student was seldom home anymore.

The notion of fleeing to Mii-chan's house crossed her mind briefly, but she soon abandoned the idea. If just Mother were home it wouldn't matter, but with Father there it would be risky. When he found out she was gone, for starters he would blame her mother, then forego his evening bath to sit waiting for her to come home so he could tongue-lash her without mercy, leaving long-lasting scars. He was after all a master at inflicting emotional pain.

Anyway, it was undoubtedly his secretary, Miss Yamane, who arranged his schedule so that now and then he could have a family dinner. Sakiko calmed her inner turmoil and shakiness with this thought.

Yoshi, the maid, polished the veranda while the gardener walked around the house with his eyes peeled, making sure that all was in order. He checked that not a speck of litter lay between the gate and the front door, raked the gravel carefully to even its surface, and sprinkled the big garden stones with water. They shone darkly, waiting for the ceremony to begin. Since Morimasa normally came home late at night, none of these things usually met his inspection.

"Be sure not to upset your father."

The mouth is the root of disaster; be silent. Their mother had drilled this into Sakiko and her sisters and generally followed her own advice, but for once she went around repeating herself. She wasn't happy that Morimasa would be home for dinner. When she found out, she'd muttered "That Yamane is a damn busybody" and hastily canceled her own plans. She'd been in a foul mood ever since. Sakiko reflected that there was no need for this constant warning. Even without being told, she and her sisters wouldn't do anything horrible. Didn't their mother know how terrified they all were of him? Didn't she realize that all their lives they'd been told not to upset their father, so many times that the words were firmly engraved in their hearts?

The car horn sounded lightly, the signal that he had arrived. Sakiko's heart thudded. Everyone in the house ran to the entranceway and knelt in fixed positions. Beside the beautifully pruned pine tree the gardener stood at attention, head bared. Morimasa came through the front door accompanied by the chauffeur, who carried his briefcase. The raised floor was edged in red pine, and Morimasa seated himself there as Yoshi slipped forward to help him off with his shoes—imported black shoes that she polished every morning to a high gleam.

While the sisters waited for their father to pass majestically by, bowing so their foreheads touched the tatami, their mother stood up, took the briefcase handed from the chauffeur to Yoshi to her, and bore it inside the house. Sakiko waited patiently for Eiko and Fusako to raise their heads, following their lead, but when Father passed by in front of her she started to get up in relief. Fusako yanked the hem of her skirt and made her get back down. "Idiot," she whispered and pinched her bottom savagely, digging in the tips of her fingernails.

Their father sat in front of the radio wearing a *yukata*, with Eiko, Fusako, Sakiko, and their mother gathered around him, all seated formally at the *kotatsu* table. Silence reigned, shrouded in a dark cloud. Into the sukiyaki pot in the center of the table went long onions, thin slices of beef, then the other ingredients, the order fixed and immutable. Eiko looked tense as she added them one by one. When she withdrew her stiff arm and let out her breath, Fusako took over with the split-second timing of a classical performing artist, adding sake, cooking wine, and soy sauce in the order prescribed for generations in the Morimoto family.

Their father's sharp, watchful eyes were like those in a photograph Sakiko had once seen of a hawk hunting its prey. The rest of them sat bolt upright, tracking his every reaction. As Fusako sprinkled in sugar and stirred carefully after each addition, he spoke approvingly:

"That's the way. If you add the ingredients like that, the flavor spreads equally throughout. You're a bright child, Fusako."

If she showed too much pleasure, it would spoil his mood. He disliked exaggerated displays. Still, to show no pleasure at all after receiving such praise wouldn't do, so Fusako curved her closed lips in a slight, decorous smile. Her eyes remained fearful, but as her father continued to look benignly on her she strove to maintain her decorous smile.

"That should do it. Go ahead and eat. If the meat cooks too long, it gets tough." At their father's words the sisters all picked up their chopsticks and reached toward the pot in the middle of the table. They were each afraid of upsetting their father by being too slow or too swift; Eiko controlled the timing of their movements. When a too-large fragment of thinly-sliced beef caught on Sakiko's chopstick, Eiko glared at her, making her hand flutter as she hastily tried to remove it.

"Bad manners. Don't poke at your food." Her father's reprimand was immediate. Sakiko's hand froze, and her eyes swam as she desperately sought help that was not forthcoming.

Eyes downcast, the girls continued slowly with the meal, keeping a weather eye on one another lest someone else make a mistake. Sakiko wanted a drink of water, but decided not to do anything uncalled for. Their mother looked relieved, but just then their father's sharp voice rang out.

"Can't you enjoy your meal? Children shouldn't act like grownups, always afraid of what someone may think. Act your age. Say something!"

Their mother's cold, determined eyes rested on Eiko, as if to say, "You're the only one who can get us through this." If Eiko remained silent, she might suffer some horrible retaliation afterward from their mother. Controlling her panic, Eiko looked up and began to talk.

"Yesterday at school the teacher spoke to us. He said that Japan has started to recover from the war, but we all have our work cut out for us. He said a woman's job is to marry, have children, and be a good wife and a sensible mother, making a warm home where her husband can relax and be at ease when he comes home tired from work. I completely agree."

Her father's gaze softened approvingly as it rested on her. "That's an admirable teacher," he pronounced.

Fusako seized the moment to say, "I'm going to be an admirable bride."

"Are you now? An admirable bride, eh?" He broke into a smile, and the tension in the room eased.

"Me, too. I want to be an admirable..." Sakiko wanted to speak up, but she abandoned the idea, cowering at the mere thought of her father thundering, "Enough! Don't keep saying the same thing as other people."

Arms folded, their father Morimasa surveyed the table, reverted to a stern expression, and shifted the topic to his philosophy of business management. This speech always began and ended with the same words: "Women and children don't understand." There was no point in telling any of this to his "women and children," he meant, but since all he had was daughters, he had no choice. Their father's bitter regret came through loud and clear, making all of them want to disappear.

The radio began chiming the signal for the start of the seven o'clock news. With the predictability of Pavlov's dog, they all sat up straight, folded their hands in their laps, and fell silent. No noise whatever was allowed during this time. Morimasa's facial muscles tightened and a blue vein stood out; his severe eyes focused on a point in space as he concentrated on the news. Anyone who made the slightest rustle would be snapped at. Rigid with tension, the sisters prayed fervently that no news disturbing to their father would come up.

After dinner, once Morimasa retired to his room, their mother took a bath and sought refuge in her room. Eiko put her sisters to bed, helped the maid tidy the kitchen, made sure the doors were all locked, and so ended her day.

Sakiko waited until everyone was quietly asleep before getting up and sneaking into the room where her father's suit hung from the lintel. She took out his wallet from the inner pocket and removed a number of thousand-yen bills before putting it back. The more often she did this, the more skillful she became. The feel of the bills and of the soft leather wallet her father handled every day were indescribably pleasant. She wanted the money, but the thrill of taking it was even better.

This is my private communication with my father. I'm the only one who has this special connection with him, she thought, caressing the soft leather steeped in her father's scent.

5 Car Accident

Through the open door of the hospital room she had finally located came the sound of someone screeching at the top of her lungs. Sakiko set her suitcase down in the hallway, gave it a kick, and stood in the doorway. The ward was crowded with beds, and in the middle stood a woman with abundant black hair and tattoos on her brown skin, waving her arms and jabbering. It was hard to tell if she was angry or jubilant. She wasn't Mexican. This was New York, so she was probably Puerto Rican. The others were all black or Asian, no whites. All were too engrossed in their own affairs to pay Sakiko any attention. Her nostrils were assailed by the mingled smells of many races and of the poor.

Sakiko looked around the room, searching for her sister Hiroko.

The hospital had telephoned Sakiko in Los Angeles: "Do you know Hiroko Morimoto? She says she is your sister. She was injured in a car accident and has been admitted to the hospital." Paul's works were being exhibited in Boston, and Hiroko had set out by herself to drive to the opening, but before ever leaving Manhattan she had gotten in an accident. Sakiko left Hideto with Ryoko and rushed to her sister's side.

Hiroko was lying asleep in a bed by the door, an intravenous tube in her arm. The Puerto Rican woman had been so distracting that Sakiko failed to see what was right in front of her. Though no doubt drugs had something to do with it, her sister's ability to sleep through the racket seemed miraculous. Marveling, Sakiko sat in a bedside chair and heard a raspy, metallic sound. She looked in that direction and saw a cockroach creeping across the floor.

The springs of the mattress were worn out and Hiroko lay sunken, her face pale and her lips purple. Of her normal self-defensiveness there was no sign. She was pathetically defenseless.

A nurse came to change the IV bag. Sakiko said, "I am her sister. I'd like to speak to her doctor and find out how she's doing." The nurse glanced at her, smiled slightly, and left the room without a word. Sakiko thought of following after her, but was immobilized by timidity.

Hiroko slightly opened her eyelids. Recognizing Sakiko, she said immediately, as if this were the only thing on her mind, "Hurry and get me a private room."

The woman behind the counter looked suspicious. "What'd you say?"

"I want to put my sister in a private room," Sakiko repeated.

The woman made a gesture of disbelief, and heaved an exaggerated sigh. "Do you have any idea how much a private room costs?"

"No. But…" I can pay, Sakiko started to say, but the woman cut her off in a stinging tone.

"I bet you don't. You have no idea, and that's why you can

ask such a thing." She informed her of the price of a private room in the aggravated tone a mother might use to tell a child begging for sweets, *Now will you be quiet?* Then over Sakiko's shoulder she called to the next person in line: "Can I help you?"

Someone from the gallery exhibiting Paul's paintings came and served as guarantor, so Hiroko was finally able to move to a private room. She slept through it all. When she awoke, she surveyed her new quarters and murmured, "This is awful. Don't they have anything better?"

"This is the best they have," said Sakiko, irritated.

The hospital where Hiroko had been brought was for low-income patients, so there was no help for it. If you were Asian, without affiliation or insurance, then even if you drove a luxury car this was the level of hospital they put you in.

"Where's Paul?" asked Hiroko, seemingly perplexed at his absence.

"I phoned and managed to get hold of him in the gallery, but I ran out of coins and we were cut off."

"Why didn't you call collect?" Hiroko had been lying listlessly in bed, but suddenly she spoke with energy.

"Well, it's the gallery phone. It didn't seem right."

"God, how have you managed to survive this long?"

As Hiroko said this in an appalled tone, lip curled, she looked so much like Fusako that Sakiko shuddered. To calm her sister down, she brought up an old memory: "Remember the time Fusako got in an accident and went in the hospital?"

"Stop being sentimental about old times." Hiroko was brusque. She glanced at the crisp rice crackers Sakiko had brought. "Those things make me feel all dried out. That's what's wrong with Japanese people—they eat things like that."

With a gesture that said *If you don't want them then I'll help myself,* Sakiko took one, put it in her mouth, and crunched it under Hiroko's baleful gaze. Then an idea hit her. "You haven't

117

contacted the branch manager yet, have you? That's who we should have asked to help with changing the room. I'll go give him a ring right now." She jumped up, feeling guilty about not having contacted anyone in the branch office of their father's company, but Hiroko stopped her with vehemence.

"Don't! You mustn't call there, absolutely not." After waiting to see Sakiko sink back into her chair, she went on. "Ever since I said I wanted to get my driver's license, they've had their minds made up I was going to get in an accident. You can't let them know, you just can't. If you do, I'll be furious."

Hiroko's pale face lost even more color, turning a ghastly hue. *So this is the color of her pride,* Sakiko thought.

As Sakiko prepared to leave, Hiroko told her, "When you hear from Paul, tell him to come right away. This is a white people's world, so without him I'm—" she started to say *all alone,* and amended it to "up a tree."

Back in Hiroko's apartment, Sakiko called Eiko and told her about the accident.

"Oh really. So she's driving. However did she manage to get her license? The examiner who passed her is a dimwit." She laughed out loud, as if impressed at having called an American a dimwit. Eiko, mother of two, was pretty cool.

"I'll tell Mother and Father," Eiko went on. "You talk to the doctor tomorrow, and if anything's seriously wrong—I'm not saying it will be, of course—then let me know. And tell Miss Yamane about the expenses." She spoke quickly, making her points with vigor. She went on to say and hear what had to be said and heard and then, because overseas calls were expensive and the charge would be exorbitant, she hung up.

Sakiko called Ryoko to find out how Hideto was, complaining at the same time about the hospital's treatment of them and the various forms of discrimination they had suffered.

Ryoko was philosophical. "We're a minority, so what do you expect? And you're oversensitive, honey. You overreact. That just makes it harder on you. Those people have their own problems, believe me. Try to understand and you'll feel better. Hideto's happy, so take your time and look after your sister all you want."

Was her indignation a sign of oversensitivity? Or was she angry at herself for not being able to handle that woman? Or was it her roots in the privileged class that made discrimination so hard for her to accept? Sakiko mulled it over, her mind going in circles.

The doctor, a white guy who exuded moroseness at being a loser still employed at this hospital, talked to Sakiko about her sister's condition. She had suffered mere bruising. The lab reports came back negative. So did that mean she could go home as soon as she was able to get about? The doctor swallowed his words, making it hard for Sakiko to catch what he was saying. Unable to quiz him, she kept repeating "Yes, yes," until the nurse called "Next!" and she walked out into the hallway, feeling as if she'd been grabbed by the scruff of the neck and tossed out. She returned to Hiroko's room, passing through sour vapors given off by people sitting against the wall.

"How was it?"

"Fine. Your test results are all negative."

Hiroko's eyes urged her to go on. But Sakiko, lacking confidence that she'd understood the mumbling doctor, remained silent.

"Ask that man from the gallery to come back and talk to him."

Sakiko nodded, knowing full well she lacked the courage. The art dealer who came the other day had been clearly put out at the imposition. She couldn't help remembering their father Morimasa's admonition, "Never cause trouble for others."

119

"Hurry up and phone him!" Irritated at Sakiko's failure to move, Hiroko tried to sit up and let out a scream of pain. The persistent, maudlin wail stripped away her sister's veneer of rationality. As it went on, Sakiko thought in surprise, *Not even I, the weakest of the four of us, would ever act this way.*

On the afternoon of the day before Hiroko was to be discharged, her door swung open and in came Paul, carrying a travel bag and a tube with a painting rolled inside. At his positive air, the sisters' faces brightened. Sakiko rushed to embrace him, and as they hugged, he said, "Hiroko, you look great!" He sounded like someone at a party who had spotted an old acquaintance and called out a greeting over a friend's shoulder.

Hiroko opened her arms wide, looking almost cheerful enough to jump out of bed. His entrance worked magic.

Sakiko's joy did not last. Knowing she was incapable of saying no, Paul asked her to pick up a present for Hideto and take it to Hiroko's apartment. The item he specified was at a toy store on Fifth Avenue, which was closer to the apartment than the hospital, and as he said, she might as well go back to the apartment from there.

Leaving gay-spirited Hiroko behind, Paul walked her to the elevator. "I'll fly back to LA in the morning," he said. "I'll take care of the paperwork here as best I can. There's Hideto to think of, though, so I should get back." What had happened to his slogan, *Let Ryoko do it?* Wondering, Sakiko looked up with a touch of bitterness at his animated face.

I feel forlorn, but Hiroko is even more forlorn than me. She should have a friend she could turn to at a time like this, instead of relying on her baby sister's husband. "Your sister Hiroko is great, smart, brave, it's a shame she's a girl!" All the things she'd been told about Hiroko all her life seemed untrue.

Sakiko tipped the doorman, who had brought everything up to Hiroko's apartment. His brown, angular face sticking out of a stiff uniform collar crinkled in gratitude. After thanking her he said, "Your sister's a real nice lady. Friendly as can be." Her sister, the one who was always touting theories of black inferiority? And yet she did once have a black maid who mothered her, and the first time Sakiko had ever seen her cry was at that performance by John Coltrane, who was also black. There was a disconnect between Hiroko's head and heart, Sakiko decided as she watched the doorman leave.

This was the first time she had ever come back to the apartment so early. She walked around taking another look at the place. Not that there was much to see besides Hiroko's artwork and books, which were everywhere. The hallway was stuffed with works she'd cleared out of the guest bathroom the day Sakiko arrived; you had to turn sideways to get through. That would be impossible for Hiroko, so soon after getting out of the hospital. Sakiko set about rearranging things to make it easier to get around.

There was a combination kitchen-dining table, so big that it was a marvel Hiroko had ever managed to fit it in the available space. No doubt she'd gone to a furniture store and bought the first item she saw, not stopping to consider the size of the room. Sakiko piled up the books scattered all over the table and cleared a place for her dinner. Then, to clear another place for Paul, she added more books to the pile, and it collapsed. Of the two chairs, one was full to the limit. She checked under the table, but that space was full of books too. The last time she came, things hadn't been this bad. Why on earth didn't Hiroko rent a place big enough to serve as a studio, even if it wasn't in quite as safe a neighborhood? For all the talking she did about her art, her way of going about it was pretty artless, Sakiko thought, smiling wryly to herself.

There was the sound of a key in the lock, and Paul came in. Sakiko flinched to think he had a key of his own, even though of course it was only natural since he stayed here on trips to New York.

Smelling of wine and garlic, he explained cheerfully that he'd had dinner with the art dealer.

"Then you didn't stay long with Hiroko?" Sakiko asked.

"Nope," he said, and yawned.

"I can't talk to you," Hiroko used to complain. "You and I aren't on the same wavelength." She'd surely been looking forward to a stimulating, intellectual conversation with Paul, so she must have been disappointed.

Paul took a shower. As he was toweling his hair dry, as if rubbing his head had given him an idea, he said, "Now's our chance. Let's sleep in Hiroko's bed!"

She hesitated momentarily, and he grabbed her by the hand and pulled with unexpected strength, as if dragging an unwilling child to an amusement park ride. The bed was all made up, ready for Hiroko. Surely when she came home she wouldn't like it if others had slept there, even if they were family. Paul's gesture of insistent, devilish glee made her feel this was not just rude but wrong somehow, sinful. At the bedroom entrance she resisted for a second, but something in her core that could not say no propelled her forward.

Morning light spilled between the curtains. She heard Paul in the shower. Naked, Sakiko slipped a dressing robe over her shoulders and opened the curtains. Then she went back to the bed, meaning to make it up as nicely as she could, and was horrified by what met her eyes. Lit up by the unfeeling rays of the morning sun, there on the navy-striped sheet was a big stain. There was no hiding it. She changed the bedding, using the floral fitted sheet on the futon where Paul was supposed to have slept, but couldn't find a matching sheet for the top. Fortunately the top sheet wasn't dirty, but its navy stripes clashed with the pink and yellow flowers. She did a swift calculation and realized that taking time to wash the stained sheet and dry it in the dryer would make them late picking up Hiroko at the hospital.

"How many roads do you have to walk down…" Paul emerged from the bathroom singing Bob Dylan's "Blowin' in the Wind." "What's wrong?" he asked, and laughed away her concern. "She'll never even notice the difference between stripes and flowers."

Sakiko left Hiroko standing by the door while she flew over to the bed and quickly turned down the covers. She fluffed up the pillow, patted the sheet, and led Hiroko over.

As Hiroko got in bed, she noticed that the bed wasn't made up the way the maid did it and the top and bottom sheets didn't match. "While I was in the hospital the maid didn't come and so you made the bed up yourself, didn't you, Sakiko?" she said graciously.

Sakiko's arm jerked. "No, she came," she said, trying to hide a quaver in her voice. Bothered by that sign of fear, Hiroko stretched out, bed-making no longer a concern. Sakiko muttered something and fled.

Hiroko thought it over. Sakiko had always been a little mouse, following closely in her sisters' footsteps. Living in the United States would teach her to be more self-assertive, Hiroko had hoped, but from the disgraceful way she'd handled herself in the hospital, clearly she hadn't changed. That's what came of being sheltered by Paul in a warm and cozy environment.

Hiroko pulled the covers up to her face. *Phew, what a smell!* Paul had slept here. Sakiko too, no doubt. Then why not come out and say so? Sakiko assumed Hiroko would be mad if she found out the two of them had slept here. Why shouldn't a married couple sleep in the same bed? As a child Sakiko was always getting yelled at by Fusako and cowering. To this day she lived in fear of others.

But oh God, the smell. She'd been glad yesterday when Paul helped her with the paperwork to be released from the hospital, but then he'd run off, saying he had a dinner appointment with an art dealer. He'd promised to put in a good word for her and her portfolio, but to her surprise she realized that she actually didn't care. Finding a place to showcase her works mattered less to her now than being with him, a development that was so pathetic it made her mad. She felt no vulgar sort of jealousy. More than the realization that they had slept in her bed, what depressed her was knowing that while she'd been alone in her hospital bed, Sakiko had been with him.

Sakiko stood stiff as a board, watching while Hiroko took the towel she'd requested, laid it over the top of her covers, and sniffed it.

"I'm going to take a nap, so leave me be," Hiroko ordered, and went on thinking.

That child won't do anything unless someone gives her an order. She can't think for herself or take action on her own. As she lay in bed idly planning to teach Sakiko the necessity of thought, Hiroko's injury continued to hurt. The pain siphoned her awareness, keeping her brain from functioning at a higher level. She felt disgusted with herself, as if she had grown stupid. Maybe this was why she'd acted so sentimental around Paul yesterday, willing him to stay. With emotion in the lead and rational thought gone stagnant, she felt she had no existential value. If she went on like this, there would be no point in living.

✳

Eiko was on the phone, repeating "Yes" like a prize pupil responding to the teacher, but gradually, as Sakiko could hear from the kitchen, her tone wavered. Wondering what was wrong, she peeked out.

Eiko's face was ashen. "Fusako has been in an accident!" Her voice was nearly a scream. Their mother, Sadako, was out again. Sakiko could only stand stock still and stare at Eiko, who was trembling.

Eiko drank some of the water offered to her by a maid, let out her breath, and wiped her cloudy glasses on the sleeve of her blouse as she related what she had just heard from Miss Yamane, the secretary.

"It's not serious, apparently. She crashed into a guard rail and was taken to the hospital." With their mother constantly out, Eiko had to take her place, and she had a strong tendency to overreact.

Following instructions from their father passed on by Miss Yamane, Sakiko and Eiko took the train to the hospital.

As Hiroko happened to be in her room upstairs, Eiko had invited her along, but she'd barely taken her nose out of her book long enough to reply. "What difference would it make if I did? Whether two of us go or three, it's all the same." She was dreadfully irritated at having her reading interrupted. Even so, Eiko answered, "Fusako would be glad to see you." At that, Hiroko looked them both straight in the eye. "I don't believe in that sort of family love," she said. "We may be a family, but we each have to live on our own. Take responsibility for our own actions. I don't object to you two going, but properly speaking, Fusako ought to sit alone and recapitulate her accident." Eiko had led the way down stairs, shaking her head in disbelief at Hiroko's "properly speaking" and "recapitulate."

"It's like she cares more about her book than about Fusako," commented Sakiko in the train. "Mm-hmm," said Eiko, her mind elsewhere. With excitement she opened the box of Chinese dumplings they had just bought at Yokohama Station, took one out, and stuffed it in her mouth. A front tooth was missing where the other day, for the first time in a while, their mother had hit her in the face.

After eating half the dumpling, scarcely realizing what she was doing, Eiko came to herself and stole a look around the car. None of the other passengers seemed to have noticed this breach of etiquette, so she relaxed, offered the box to Sakiko, and began to talk.

"Why do you suppose our family is so scattered? Hiroko's always out somewhere or cooped up in her room, and Fusako seems to have made some bad friends in college and does nothing but run around with them. Mother is never home. When I have a family, I want it to be cheerful and warm. You know, like Sazae in the comics." She looked entranced, as if she could see the Isono family living room reflected in the train window.

Uncertain how to reply, Sakiko looked from her sister's face to the dumplings and back again.

"Anyway," Eiko went on, "aren't these dumplings yummy? I'm sorry for Fusako and everything, but I'm glad to be able to eat them." She beamed, and Sakiko beamed back, relieved at the change of topic. The sisters traded happy looks, their cheeks stuffed with dumplings.

Fusako had gone to stay overnight with a friend in Kugenuma, and while driving her friend's car had gotten into an accident. When she first heard this, Sakiko thought, *I wonder who Fusako's friend is. For a long time now she's acted like she doesn't want to be around me and just gone off by herself. I'm busy studying for entrance exams so I don't have time to play, but she could at least talk to me. Instead she avoids me... I wonder, why didn't she die? If it was me, I wouldn't just get in an accident,*

I'd go on and die. I don't know what death is like but anything would be better than this suffering and pain.

As she stood on the station platform, the breeze from a passing train gently brushed the softness of her breast. It felt vaguely like an invitation to the next world. When that happened, she longed to disappear.

"Sakiko, aren't you going to eat any more?" At the sound of her sister's insistent urging, Sakiko came to herself. The last dumpling was wavering apprehensively in the box. Eiko was unwilling to relinquish it, but unless she let her younger sister have it, she would lose face as the one who had taken on the role of substitute mother. All this was written large on her face, so Sakiko picked up the dumpling in her fingers and popped it in her mouth. If Fusako were here, she would scold, "It's bad manners to eat with your fingers!" She always added mean things that amounted to total rejection: *You can't do anything right, you piece of trash, you moron!* Normally Eiko would have said "Use your chopsticks," but she was so busy trying to think what to say when they got there that she didn't notice.

"A woman drive a car?" yelled their father, Morimasa. "Out of the question! She'd be damaged goods, unmarriageable!"

Fusako had told Sakiko, "You ask, they'll listen to you," and so Sakiko had dialed her sister's friend to ask permission for her to drive their car. Morimasa had happened to be sleeping off a cold, and heard the phone conversation. He tore out of his room and stood fiercely at the top of the stairs, arms akimbo.

He was terrifying. Still holding the receiver, Sakiko wet her pants.

Their mother, Sadako, already in a bad mood from having to give up her plans for the evening with Father home, poked her head out of the living room and scowled at the sight of the puddle on the floor in the hallway. "Tae, wipe that up," she said to the maid, and slammed the door shut again.

Sakiko thrust her feet into a pair of wooden clogs by the veranda and rushed in tears to Mii-chan's house.

She threw open the front door with a clatter.

"Sakiko, is that you?" called a voice, and Mii-chan's mother came running. "I knew it was you, Sakiko!" she said with evident joy. "I could tell by the sound. You haven't come by very often since you started high school, and I've missed you. Oh, it's so good to see you! Hurry, come on in!"

She grasped Sakiko by the hand, her hand encircling Sakiko's with a warmth that seemed to emanate from deep within her, and led her into the living room.

The ordinary but polished wooden cabinet, which along with the house had survived the fires of war, was covered with patchwork that Mii-chan's mother had made by sewing together tiny squares of cloth. The cushions on the well-cleaned tatami mats were patchwork, too. The tears in the fusuma sliding doors were repaired with a clever arrangement of paper in many colors and shapes. On the tea table were wildflowers arranged in an empty can.

Mii-chan's mother's approach to life was the same as ever: she simply enjoyed being alive.

When she was little, Sakiko had spent more time here than at her own home. She used to kick off her shoes and rush inside shouting *"Kontada,"* a mixture of *konnichiwa* (hello) and *tadaima* (I'm home). But after she started junior high, she couldn't do that anymore.

"Sit down, sit down!" urged Mii-chan's mother, but with her wet pants Sakiko couldn't, so she just stood and squirmed. "What is it?" said Mii-chan's mother, peering kindly into her face. "You look troubled." The warm words brought a flood of relief, and Sakiko began to sniffle. Little by little, in answer to the older woman's questions, she told how terrifying her father was.

"I see. You were really frightened, weren't you? Poor thing." Mii-chan's mother hugged her so tight it hurt. Sakiko grabbed at her kindness.

Sakiko had always been saved this way by this woman. Mii-chan's mother was what kept her from plunging into the world beyond. After changing into a pair of Mii-chan's underpants, offered as matter-of-factly as if they were a handkerchief, Sakiko returned to find hot tea and homemade potato pastries on the table. "Mii-chan has gone out tutoring, and won't be back till late, but I hope you'll stay for supper. Her father and I would both be glad if you did."

It was nice to be asked, but with Father home, this was impossible. Too bad, because the moment when Mii-chan's mother said, "Now, you've got to eat up!" and put some of her own food on top of Sakiko's rice was sheer bliss. At home, nobody wanted to hear about her day, but here she could talk on and on, and Mii-chan's mother would listen with evident enjoyment, nodding or laughing or showing surprise. Sometimes she would chide, "That's not right! You mustn't do such things." And then, calmly and gently, she would explain. The sight of Mii-chan chatting with her father, nodding along as he spoke, the two of them sharing surprise and laughter, made Sakiko blindly jealous.

I wish I could talk to my father like that, she thought, and one day she said so to Mii-chan's mother. The older woman leaned her head to one side on her slender neck and stared into space, thinking. Finally she turned to Sakiko and said, "Well then, Sakiko, how about this? Why don't you make it your goal to have a conversation with your father someday? I know you can do it."

"You think so?" Sakiko said in a tiny voice.

"Of course! I know you can do it, and your father knows it,

too. But he's very busy now, and that makes him so tired that he can't show you how he feels, that's all."

Never before had anyone said such a thing to her: "I know you can do it." Sakiko repeated the words to herself and felt a burst of confidence.

"Okay," she said.

When Sakiko and Eiko peered in the hospital room, Fusako, who'd been asleep, studied them with bleary eyes as if to say, "What are you two doing here?"

"Mr. Shirataki is coming to pick us up tomorrow, so he said we should spend the night here." Mr. Shirataki was their father's chauffeur.

Fusako looked worried. "If Father sends Mr. Shirataki here, what will *he* do? Use a hired car? I'm causing poor Father so much trouble..." Tears filled her eyes.

"It's all right, Miss Yamane will take care of everything." Eiko brought out the box of dumplings she had saved for Fusako, took one out and popped it in Fusako's mouth. *Now doesn't that taste good? Just try and tell me it doesn't!* her smile seemed to say.

Seeing that Fusako and Sakiko were chatting quietly for once, Eiko slipped out of the room, went to the store and exchanged some money for a pile of ten-yen coins. She called the owner of the smashed car. Miss Yamane had already been in contact with her and made all the necessary arrangements. At a loss to know how to respond to the fluent protestations of the lady on the other end of the line—"We have received so much kindness beyond all reason that I really feel quite mortified"—Eiko bowed her head again and again. She came back muttering about how her neck hurt, and got Sakiko to rub her shoulders. "Mother never says anything at times like this, so how am I supposed to know what to say?" she complained. "Mother thinks you can always express your appreciation with things."

"So it was Miss Yamane who arranged for Fusako's private room."

"Yes. If it wasn't for her, what would become of us? Seriously."

After saying the word "Seriously" with emphasis, Eiko looked around the nearly-empty car, making sure her words would not carry to the other passengers before continuing.

"This is a secret. Don't tell. Promise?"

Hastily Sakiko nodded, wondering what this could be leading up to. Eiko began to talk, lowering her voice.

"I'm worried. I'm really glad that Miss Yamane serves as a pipeline between Father and us. But..." She looked straight at Sakiko, wavered, then plunged on. "Father...they say Father sometimes makes decisions at work that no one can understand. Like, remember Mr. Asai, that executive? Every New Year's he always used to bring us those cakes we liked so much. Well, this year he didn't come, did he? He got fired. You know why?" Eiko took a deep breath. "Because he took the day off on his wedding anniversary. He got fired for that."

Imagining her father Morimasa's face livid with anger, the blue vein pulsating, Sakiko shivered. Eiko watched her and went on without a pause.

"It's the same with company advertising. When a man produced something that Father had preapproved, he took one look, flew into a rage, and fired the poor man. And at meetings, everyone just listens to what Father already decided, but once someone said what he thought and was fired on the spot. They say just looking doubtful is enough to get you demoted. The employees are like chessmen, and Father is the only one who can move them around. So there's nothing but sycophants left in the whole company."

For a moment, biting her lip, Eiko showed such anxiety that the train window frosted over. "Sakiko," she said, "I'm so worried that Father may get upset at Miss Yamane and fire her for taking things into her own hands. She does so much for us, always looking out for us, but nobody knows what he thinks about it. Anything could happen."

This outburst from Eiko, who normally never talked about their father this way, surprised Sakiko and reminded her of what Hiroko had said: "Father is always issuing a command in the morning and reversing it at night, but no one knows the thought process in between. Act surprised, and he lashes out. Nothing makes any sense, so there's nothing to do but hold him in fear. Tremble at his words. That's the source of his charisma. The classic example of a company founder."

6 "Go on and cry!"

The car with Hiroko in it was crossing the bridge. The Manhattan skyline was behind them; they seemed to be heading toward Brooklyn, not that it mattered. Shizuko, the one person in this great metropolis with whom Hiroko had any association, was at the wheel. This was the station wagon of the shop she worked for. Ever since the accident, Hiroko had given up driving. Although perhaps it would be more accurate to say that her father, Morimasa, had ordered her to give it up.

She felt listless. Suddenly she broke out in a sweat. Her hair, even though cut short, was soaking wet from the tip to the scalp, and sweat trickled down her forehead. Her underwear was soaking too. When she told her doctor, he'd said it was "change of life" and prescribed strong tranquilizers and sleeping medication.

She hadn't painted for a long time now. She'd put an end to that meaningless activity. Throwing away her finished paintings was too much trouble, so she dumped them in the room that used to be her studio.

One day last year, a letter had come from Morimasa. He wrote that he had received the announcement of a group exhibition containing paintings of Hiroko's. Was there no solo exhibition yet? How many years had she been in New York now? "I don't want all the money I've invested in you to go to waste," he warned. "I've never made a bad investment yet, but now it seems my own daughter has failed me; a woman can't make the grade after all." The fierce black words written in calligraphy on her father's favorite handmade paper had stabbed Hiroko in the eyes. Her heart wrenched. She sweated from head to toe.

Ever since, whenever she picked up a brush those words appeared on the canvas. She tried to paint, but was overcome by misgivings: what was the use? She began to feel that way not only when trying to paint, but at ordinary times. She was consumed with self-reproach over having let down the father she adored.

Paul never contacted her anymore on his trips to New York. When he stopped staying at her apartment, Sakiko apologized. She gave Hiroko the number of the place where he was staying and urged her to phone him. *Why should I,* wondered Hiroko, *when he doesn't call me? I have my pride. She's too stupid to understand that.*

"We're there! Out of the car."

Startled by Shizuko's voice, Hiroko came to herself and rattled the door, which wouldn't open. Terrified at the prospect of being shut inside, she sweated again. Shizuko reached over and lifted the stud on the door. Her cold, over-the-shoulder look and mocking words cut Hiroko to the quick: "What is it, Your Highness, amnesia? Forgot how to open a car door?"

An orderly street lined with brownstone buildings. Old-fashioned streetlamps. A man in a tailored coat with the collar turned up, back straight, walking a large dog. No one else in sight. Just ahead, as Hiroko went forward with Shizuko holding her by the arm, one light clashed with those around it, somehow vulgar and boorish.

She went down several stone steps, pushed open a door with peeling paint in a sordid shade of light blue, and went inside. There was a strong smell of cigarette smoke and something else, like burning weeds. She froze, appalled by the shabby appearance of the performers in the back of the huge room. A red-shirted man who'd been chatting with the bartender across the empty room came over with his arms opened wide and gave Shizuko a hug. The players smiled hello.

This place is cheap, miserable, and moldy, thought Hiroko. *What was she thinking, bringing me to a low-class joint like this? It can only depress me more. This is nothing like the place I heard Coltrane play. I'm only here because I associated the word "jazz" with him.* Dragging her feet, tense with anger, Hiroko sat in the seat she was shown to.

During intermission, the young white guy playing bass dropped by their table. A worn corduroy jacket, dirt-stained jeans. "Hi, honey," he said in a husky voice, placing a hand on Shizuko's shoulder as he settled gracefully in a broken chair and pulled a pack of cigarettes from a jacket pocket dark with grime. Judging from the way he carried himself, he did not come from a bad family, Hiroko thought.

"This is Hiroko, my best friend. This is Charlie, the best bassist around." Shizuko's nails, red polish peeling, waved to the left and right, and the man named Charlie turned toward Hiroko with a relaxed smile on his pale, dried-up face. He gave off a warmth that touched her in spite of herself.

Charlie took turns sipping his whiskey and water and taking drags on his cigarette, his thin body swaying.

"Hiroko is an artist," Shizuko told him. "She does the most wonderful paintings. And she's the daughter of a millionaire."

She made the last comment with wicked pleasure, grinning to see Hiroko's face stiffen.

"Really," said Charlie in a muffled voice, with a glance at Hiroko. Behind the blunt gesture something flashed, the familiar response people had on first learning she'd been born into wealth.

Shizuko, who had observed this, said, "Charlie's interested in art. You should show him your paintings, Hiroko."

He was standing in front of her door, swaying. Wearing a self-protective smile like a seawall, he slid fearful eyes past Hiroko, his gaze darting worriedly around the room behind her.

An unexpected visit.

Mute with nervousness, Hiroko motioned him inside. He drifted past her and sat on the living room sofa, legs fully extended. His movements had a strange elegance.

"What would you like to drink?"

"Whiskey and water," he said promptly. "No ice." After fishing in his pockets he produced a crumpled pack of cigarettes, drew one out, and lit it.

"Nice place," he said, and then laughed out loud as if embarrassed at the remark. The setting sun, brightening for a last moment before it disappeared, lit up his face. His skin was lusterless, wrinkled. Shizuko had said he was in his early twenties, but to Hiroko he looked older.

He picked up a copy of *The Catcher in the Rye* left out on the table and became absorbed in the page he opened to. While he read, his cigarette and drink went untouched.

Returning the book to the table, he said solemnly, "My bible."

Paul had brought it over. Hiroko had tried a number of times to read the book, but always tossed it aside midway. "This isn't literature," she would say, and he would reply with irony, "It's too hard for you to understand."

"It's not literature," she said, looking Charlie in the eye.

"That's a queer thing to say." He laughed again. "You're a funny lady."

Controlling her anger, Hiroko gave him a quick quiz on literature and the arts. Emily Brontë. Faulkner. Proust and Dostoyevsky. Jackson Pollack. To her surprise, he knew quite a bit. Impressively well-read, and well-versed in the arts, too, with ready responses for the high-level questions she posed. No mere musician he. He passed the test.

When the newly-opened bottle of whiskey was about half gone, he took out a narrow, hand-rolled cigarette and lit it. Took a deep drag and held it in. This was what she'd smelled on first entering the cafe where they met. Aware of her eyes on him, without opening his mouth he held out the cigarette invitingly. Enticed by the intensity of his effort to keep smoke from escaping through his nose and mouth, she reached out.

One puff and she choked. Laughing harder than ever, Charlie grabbed the cigarette back and took another quick drag, apparently loath to let any of it go to waste. His eyes were heavy-lidded. He laughed all the time, as if everything was funny. Laughed for no reason, with high amusement. What on earth was in that skinny cigarette? Her pride was wounded by something she knew nothing about.

"Got any music?" He looked around the room, wafted over to the stereo. Squatted down and pulled records from the rack, piling them between his spread knees as he examined them one by one. Now and then his body would sway and jerk, and he'd look up with a dazed expression that said *Where am I?*

"Here we go!"

The record he settled on with a shout was John Coltrane's *Giant Steps.* Hiroko had bought it shortly after going with

Sakiko to hear Coltrane perform. She'd forgotten she had it.

The sounds that had gotten beneath the surface of her soul that time came sliding inside her again. To stop them, she crossed her arms tightly across her chest. The memory was frightening. She must defend herself against that world of emotion. She crouched down and held perfectly still.

The sounds stopped.

Out in the street a car pulled up, people spoke, car doors slammed. Loneliness made her want to cling to these sounds from utter strangers.

"With all this avant-garde music, what's Coltrane doing here?" Charlie's voice broke in, as if he'd drifted back from somewhere on high.

She was silent. If she opened her mouth, something she was holding back might slip out, something beyond the realm of rationality. She held herself perfectly still, eyes downcast.

"Hiroko, you look lonely. What is it?" He got up and came closer.

She shivered. No, this was no good. Her emotions were in play. A tear slipped out and rolled down her cheek. This would never do. She stood up, propelled by her desire to keep him from seeing. He realized what she was doing.

"Did I say something wrong?"

A long silence.

Then suddenly, "Go on and cry!" he yelled. "Fucking cry all you want. Crying is joy, man."

Propelled by his strangely affirmative tone, Hiroko went into the bathroom. And sobbed, not caring how loud she was.

She thought she heard the front doorbell ring downstairs. She checked her watch; it was past eight. The rhythm of her life was different from that of her sisters, so she didn't go downstairs.

Back when she'd opened the book she was reading, the maid had come to announce dinner was ready, so they must have finished eating already. *Who could it be down there at this hour?* she wondered, returning her eyes to her book.

There was the sound of heavy feet on the stairs, and the door to Hiroko's room slid open. Two young Caucasian men in military uniforms with white helmets came in. MPs.

Hiroko had just been reading about events that took place in Manchuria after it became clear that Japan had lost the war. A Japanese girl went out into the street disguised as a Chinese, and Russian soldiers saw through her disguise and raped her. Her mind superimposed these MPs over those Russian soldiers, and she was as terror-stricken as if she were about to be torn to pieces. Somehow she managed not to scream. *Stay calm,* she told herself. *Reason trumps emotion:* this was the creed of her father, Morimasa, the creed under which she had grown up. She tried to analyze her terror, but her overwrought brain, now hot and now cold, could not comply.

Keeping her eyes down so the MPs wouldn't see how afraid she was, she straightened her back and crossed her arms with as great a look of importance as she could muster. Momentarily the thought of her sisters downstairs flashed through her mind. Eiko was there, so they'd be all right. Eiko lived for her role as substitute mother, so with her in charge, there was nothing to worry about. No one had ever asked her to take on the role—odd of her to be so devoted, Hiroko thought, trying unsuccessfully to divert herself from the scene at hand.

The MPs looked around the room. One of them picked up a copy of Emily Brontë's *Wuthering Heights* over by the window and showed it to his partner; together they flipped through the pages, staring, before the first one replaced the book, head tilted quizzically to one side. Their evident puzzlement made Hiroko's fear abate slightly. *A pair of ignoramuses who don't even know* Wuthering Heights—*if that's who they are, what is there to be afraid of? You're much better educated than they are,* she told herself. *Nothing beats intelligence, not even those pistols at their sides. If they ask you something, just reply using vocabulary so sophisticated they'll never have heard it before. They'll be so humiliated at their own ignorance, they'll pack up and leave.* Fear held her immobile. The MPs looked around the room again, glanced at her, and left the room talking to each other, using words she didn't know.

That must have been slang. Not until long afterwards did it occur to her that hearing slang in practice had been a valuable experience. At the time, suppressing the desire to burst into loud tears, she had sat rubbing the stiffness from her body, remembering with pride her father's words: "Hiroko isn't like women and children who whimper and cry. She's a very intelligent child."

There was the sound of the front door closing, and then Eiko, Fusako, and Sakiko came bursting up the stairs, fighting to be first.

"Guess what I did," said Eiko, beaming triumphantly. "Before they came I took all the cigarettes Mother bought at the PX and threw them in the closet."

Hiroko was silent, afraid that if she opened her mouth, the terror inside her would escape.

"You're an English major, so you could understand them, huh, Hiroko?" Sakiko said nonchalantly.

Seeing how little afraid her sisters were, perhaps because they'd been together, Hiroko's pride was hurt.

Fusako was oddly impressed. "Gosh, they were tall, weren't they? Blond and blue-eyed, with such white skin!"

Her sisters had no clue that anything horrible could have happened. Maybe, thought Hiroko, ignorance and lack of imagination were a blessing in the end.

*

The sound of the doorbell came from the apparatus on the kitchen wall; it ruled Hiroko's life. She used the bathroom closer to the kitchen, since the one by the bedroom made her nervous that she might not hear the doorbell. In fact, wherever she was in the apartment, she stayed on alert, all ears. The doorman, on good terms now with Charlie, no longer bothered to notify her when he came. So when the doorbell rang, Charlie was right there at her door. She took to being careful with her appearance so she'd be ready whenever he came. It seemed like a million years ago that she used to spend all day in her bathrobe.

The maid was there that day. She used to come twice a week, but to keep her from running into Charlie, Hiroko had cut it down to once a week, which was a little awkward. He didn't really come that often anyway.

"Hi, honey!" Just like always, he came in with that familiar smile on his face, the one she privately called his "seawall smile." He sat down on the living room sofa with his legs extended and lit a cigarette, waiting for her to bring him a bottle of whiskey, a glass, and some water. This, too, was the same as always.

He finished his first cigarette and brought out the mari juana. Hiroko had come to like it, and gave him money to buy it for her. She took two or three drags and had just started to get high when the maid came out. Her third since the one Sakiko had envied her. The maid twitched her flat nose and stared at the two of them wide-eyed as she picked up the scent. Charlie waved at her. "Hi, honey!" He seemed to be inviting her to join them. She ignored him and went to work in the kitchen. Before, Hiroko used to have her go shopping and do some cooking, too, but now that she came once a week she only did the cleaning and laundry.

Baseless fear kept Hiroko from going outside. The doctor said it was a symptom connected to menopause and in time it would go away. The best cure, he added, would be for her to find a boyfriend who lived far away and commute to his place.

She phoned the supermarket to have her groceries delivered. About the only times she went out were when she went to the doctor for medication and when she called at the office of an acquaintance of her father's for help with her visa. She was supposed to be working there. Someone from her father's branch office always drove her over and back.

"We need to talk," said the maid. Hiroko followed her into a back room.

"You know marijuana's illegal, don't you? You want me to call the police? You'd get arrested. They'd deport you to Japan." The maid was intimidating. Her sweaty dark skin glistened, and her reddish eyes seemed about to pop.

The threat of deportation made Hiroko's heart turn over. She started to shake. "What do you want?" she managed to say, her voice husky.

With a sneer at such ignorance, the maid said contemptuously, "Guacamole."

Hiroko went into the bedroom, took out her checkbook from the nightstand drawer, and wrote out a check for an amount in three figures. As she handed it over, she managed to say, "You needn't come back." The maid contemplated the amount with a satisfied grin, her eyes redder than ever. With fingers so thick they could easily have suffocated Hiroko if pressed around her neck, she snapped the check.

"Why in God's name would you give her so much money?" Shizuko's voice rang through the receiver. "I can't believe how naive you are! And tell me this, Your Highness—did you get her to return her key?"

The question awoke Hiroko to the fact that she had not gotten her key back.

The previous day, the maid had quickly left. "You found yourself a nice rich girlfriend," she'd told Charlie. "Squeeze her for all you can get." With this parting shot, she'd gone out the door, humming a gospel song. Charlie, listening to Coltrane with the volume high, never heard her. Even if he had, he was so high it would have sounded like mere noise.

"Before you call the manager, make sure you get rid of the smell of marijuana," Shizuko advised over the phone, stifling a laugh. Hiroko followed all her advice, starting with changing the lock.

Shizuko worked at the Oriental Lampshade, a store selling lamps made from Oriental vases that was run by a fiftyish Japanese-American man. She too had come to the United States to become a painter, but couldn't support herself that way.

"You don't have to work, so you can paint all you want." This was her constant reproach. It always made Hiroko feel guilty. Still, at least Shizuko didn't do what so many others did and cut off their friendship because of blind prejudice: *You come from a wealthy family so you're different from me,* the implied refrain went.

Hiroko called Sakiko in LA for the first time in a long while. "Shizuko recommended a new maid for me, but she's awfully expensive," she said, not going into what had happened to the old one. Sakiko had turned into such a prim and protective mommy, the mere word "marijuana" was bound to make her uptight. Paul would find out too, she thought briefly, but he no longer mattered.

"Oh really," said Sakiko, and was silent a moment. Then she said with determination, "You know, Hiroko, you look down on housework, but it's surprisingly good for your state of mind.

I used to have a Mexican woman come in, but then I decided to do everything myself. I was really surprised to find out how peaceful, how calming it is." She took a breath. "It feels like I have my feet on the ground. Of course, there are times I don't feel like doing it. And it has to be done every day. But once you get into a rhythm, it's not as bad as you think it's going to be, and there's a lot to be gained. You should give it a try. Take my word for it. If I'm wrong, you can always hire a new maid later."

She wants me to do housework. Scrub out the insides of toilets. Me? God no. She really is a little idiot. It's because I haven't made a name for myself. If I had, she'd never talk to me this way. Everybody in the family treats me with contempt, from Father on down. They think I'm a loser.

Hiroko walked away, leaving the receiver off the hook.

When Hiroko suddenly disappeared, Sakiko regretted having spoken out of line. But she didn't have the courage to call her sister back. Instead she looked out at the moon behind the redwood that bordered their property and the neighbors', a neither-this-nor-that moon, somewhere between full and half.

When had it first started? Yes, around the time Paul stopped staying at Hiroko's place on his trips to New York. Until then she used to call constantly, and then the calls abruptly stopped. If Sakiko phoned, Hiroko made it seem like an intrusion, as if she were too busy to sit around talking. When Sakiko asked, "Are you getting a lot of painting done?" she laughed sardonically. "You know the answer. Don't ask such a stupid question." Stupid, dumb, idiotic: having been heaped with abuse from Fusako in childhood, Sakiko was sensitive to such words. They hurt.

Before Paul set out for New York, she asked him why he no longer stayed at Hiroko's place, and his answer was ready-made: "I don't want to interfere with her painting." Probably the real reason was that she kept pestering him to introduce her to members of the art world, and when he did, the results weren't what she hoped. *Hiroko must be mad at Paul for being concerned only with his own career and not doing enough to help her with hers.* That would explain why he avoided her now, Sakiko thought.

Charlie brought over the record, removed it from the jacket like a holy object, laid it reverently on the turntable, and set the needle. The red jacket, patched with Scotch tape where it had worn away and torn around the edges, bore the words "Thelonious Monk" in black and white. Hiroko loved the music, starting with the unique piano solo.

"When I was little," said Charlie, "my mother brought me to New York to hear him. She was an alcoholic who loved jazz. My father was Catholic, a used-car dealer who thought only about making money. They went to high school together and got married after she got pregnant with me. I was conceived in the back seat of a car. Happens a lot."

He was taking a break with marijuana and a glass of whiskey and water.

"For high school, I went to a boys' school and had to live in a dorm. Torture. Finally I broke a bunch of rules, refused to admit the error of my ways, and got expelled. A crime of conscience. Then I came to New York—just like him." Glass in hand, he pointed to the tabletop copy of *The Catcher in the Rye* and laughed.

Hiroko's eyes lingered on the scar on his wrist, which had bothered her for some time.

"What, this? Did it while listening on the phone to my girlfriend say she wanted to call it quits." He laughed again. The sadness in his laughter passed down Hiroko's throat like an invisible line tugging on the sadness shut away inside her. She stiffened her muscles to block the way, putting up a slight resistance, but to no avail. There was an ache in her chest that she recognized as sadness. It was not unpleasant. Rather, it felt good.

Tears spilled over. Charlie's bony arms stole around her, pulling her close. She buried herself in his chest and cried, wrapped in the sour smell of his dirty sweater. This time the surfacing of emotions brought no apprehension. She felt calm; she wanted to go on feeling the pain of life itself.

The moment Hiroko was born, the atmosphere had filled with disappointment that she was a girl. The head maid had let out a sigh and said, "The master will surely be disappointed." But still Hiroko was a first child, and the atmosphere surrounding her quickly turned celebratory.

A door slid open, and Hiroko was enveloped in great peace of mind. A beautiful woman lifted her carefully with hands that shook slightly, as if fearful she might break, and presented her with a breast. This was her mother, Sadako. Maternal love penetrated Hiroko to the core, made her feel safe and protected. Held snugly in those soft, warm arms, day after day she played, cried, drank milk, slept.

One day when her mother came something was different. The moment the door opened, her mother's despondent air pierced Hiroko through. Her blood froze. Her mother's eyelids were swollen, her face was inert, and she emitted a sense of futility. The arms that picked Hiroko up were so tense they all but creaked. Hiroko was afraid of falling. The breast was all wrong, too. She sucked mightily but got only a drop of milk, then none.

Hunger made Hiroko bawl. Her mother took her breast in

her hands and tried to squeeze milk out, her face twisting in pain. Then her expression changed to one of resignation and sadness, and tears fell from her eyes. Hiroko was too frightened to cry. Seeing that she had grown quiet, her mother gave her a strange look, picked her up again and then, as if something inside had burst, began to sob. Hiroko was gripped by an unholy terror. Her muscles locked; she couldn't move.

From then on, Hiroko kept a lid on her heart. Everything she saw, heard, and felt went not down into her heart but up into her brain. That became her method of self-protection.

The doorbell rang. Hiroko ran to the door, forgetting that moments before she had told herself doing so was pitiful and had sworn "never again."

When the door closed, Charlie stood in front of it, produced two joints of marijuana from his pocket, took Hiroko by the hand and laid them on her palm with a laugh. "Today I've got work," he said, lingering. She motioned for him to come in, sit down, and have a drink before going, but he murmured he had no time, still making no attempt to leave.

Hiroko saw the light. She brought her checkbook out of the bedroom and opened it on the dining-room table, brushing dirty dishes out of the way. "How much?" she asked.

Charlie shrugged, jiggling.

"Five hundred?" she suggested.

He nodded, reddened, stuffed the check in his pocket, and barely got out a muffled "Thank you" before turning his back to her with a laugh. He laid his hand on the doorknob, then turned as if remembering something, took a step toward her and gave her a peck on the cheek. She stood stiffly erect. Her desire for him to stay fought with her pride, which found such weakness scandalous. He vanished out the door.

Next to the open checkbook lay the two joints of marijuana. Hiroko stood in stunned silence in the room piled with dirty things.

If he was going to leave like that, maybe she should have the maid come twice a week after all. The apartment would be cleaner, and she would have someone to talk to. The new maid, though also black, was attending Columbia University on a scholarship, and was educated enough to have a decent conversation with. Race was not an issue; Hiroko could not get along with people of low intelligence. *She likes my paintings: that shows how smart she is,* thought Hiroko, or rather Hiroko's pride.

The doorman's voice sounded through the intercom. "Mr. Smith, a friend of Mr. Lachappelle's, is here to see you."

"Let him in," Hiroko answered automatically. Who could it be?

It was somebody from his band. Somebody she'd met that time she went to the club in Brooklyn.

"Hi, Hiroko. It's me, John."

As Hiroko hesitated over whether to invite him in or not, he came on in, a peddler of intimacy. His arms reached out, but she stepped back to avoid his hug and instead bowed her head. She hated the Japanese custom of bowing, and even back in Japan would never do it unless instructed to by her father, but at times like this it came in handy.

He had on a cashmere coat, the kind Fifth Avenue businessmen wore, but it was filthy, and his sneakers had big tears where his toes poked through. When he removed the bowler hat from his head, a tangle of greasy hair fell to his shoulders. It smelled so awful that she took another step back.

John stood with hat in hands, rocking on his heels. "I came on an errand for Charlie, to pick up his check." His brazen way of talking, and the magic word "Charlie," made her nod.

While she wrote out a check, he peered around the room, twitching his nose like an animal in search of prey. Hiroko handed him a check on which she had written a random number. He looked at it, his blue eyes moving from left to right and back again, then all at once sparkling. He stuffed the check in his coat pocket and held out his hand. "Thank you, thank you!" He backed up and stepped into the hallway, scattering happiness as he went. Clearly he had never expected such a good outcome. Finally, with one more "Thank you" for good measure, he smiled at her radiantly and was gone. Her own spirits buoyed to think that a check could bring anyone such happiness, Hiroko forgot to ask him about Charlie.

She told Charlie about the incident as he lay stretched out on the bed with his eyes closed, listening now to Clifford Brown. "Really?" he said, exhaling marijuana smoke. From his demeanor she couldn't tell whether or not he had known. Either way, it didn't matter. One phone call and the local branch manager of her father's company would transfer more funds to her account.

The incident repeated itself. As she wrote out check after check, one day one of them bounced. She telephoned the branch manager. Unlike his usual obliging manner, his response was curt: "I have instructions from Tokyo not to transfer any more money to your account." When she asked if the instructions came from her father, he said only, "I don't know."

How dare he talk to me that way!

She phoned her father, Morimasa. The attitude of his secretary, who took the call, had changed. Until just recently her tone had harbored grudging respect for Hiroko as an artist. Now she sounded almost insolent. If only Miss Yamane were there—but she had retired, caught by the firm's women-only policy of early retirement.

Her father, when she finally got hold of him a few days later, was adamant. "Don't expect a penny more from me until you hold a solo show," he barked. When she tried to explain why she hadn't been able to do that, he said curtly, "Come home." But how could she possibly go home on such terms? She started to mention Paul's gallery as a possible venue, and her father cut her off: "Forget it," he said, and hung up.

His words had borne an air of finality. Mixed in was the insidious, irrepressible male urge to crush another's human dignity. Her father, Morimoto Morimasa, was widely admired as a man of unshakable integrity, but ever since she was a little girl Hiroko had secretly sensed the hidden darkness within him. She had tried valiantly to brush it aside, but now she could no longer do so. This was the moment when the wall of rationality she had put up in self-defense came crashing down.

"I can't write any more checks for a while," she said.

Charlie chuckled. "So what?" Today's sound was Charlie Mingus. As the sound of the bass filled crevices in the wall of her heart, Hiroko realized that she hadn't been to one of Charlie's live performances in some time.

Even after she stopped writing checks, he still came by, bringing marijuana. When she asked Shizuko to sell her jewels for her to cover her living expenses, Shizuko had ordered her to get a job.

"Don't do it," said Charlie. "There's just no point." Unusually for him, his voice was firm.

"I have to pay my utilities," she murmured, with a sense that the earth was giving way beneath her feet.

He gave her a look that said, *What a funny creature you are, to be so jumpy about a thing like that.* When she asked where to reach him, he always only chuckled. How he lived she had no idea. Probably in an apartment with a busted toilet, along with his music buddies. When he came over, his ritual was a joint followed by a whiskey and water before he climbed in the tub for an incredibly long soak. He used up a whole bar of soap and emptied her bottles of shampoo and conditioner. Wrapped luxuriously in one of the big terrycloth towels she'd bought at Saks Fifth Avenue, he stepped out heavily into the hall. Sometimes he would sink onto the living room sofa like that, or stretch out on her bed and wait for her to bring him a lighted joint.

When he left, she would be appalled that he could put his old, filthy clothes back on. It never occurred to her to wash them and dry them in the dryer.

Today while he was relaxing after his bath, he took a couple of drags on the joint and asked, "How much is the rent on this place?"

"I own it, so there is no rent."

"Sell it, then."

He said this so casually that she was taken aback.

The music of Ornette Coleman coming over the speakers, its difficulty so well suited to her taste, was also bothersome.

The process of finding and purchasing this apartment had all been handled by someone from the branch office, while Hiroko focused on her painting. She did distinctly remember being advised that she could not sell the place at her own discretion. At the time she had thought that someday, when she sold her paintings and moved into a better place, she would make the man eat those words.

"I want to sell my apartment": Hiroko phoned the branch manager and told him this. After a pause, he said, "Let me talk it over with the main office."

She wept, pleading that her electricity would be cut off if they didn't hurry, and the following day received this word: "Three hundred dollars has been transferred to your account. You have to promise not to borrow from any other institution."

When Shizuko heard all this, she marveled. "Wow, must be nice! You really are a bona fide princess. Anyways, nobody in their right mind would ever hire you, so I was out of line telling you to get a job. Everyone just laughed at me."

By "everyone" she meant the community of Japanese artists living in New York, none of whom would have anything to do with Hiroko since she was a member of the privileged class. Except the men, who came one by one in secret, to attack her. Pretending they had some urgent message to convey. While she was making tea they would come up suddenly and grab her from behind. The hasty ones among them would hand her a bag of goodies as they came at her, lips pursed for a kiss. There was no particular sequence. These men were full of energy, but either from an artist's pride or from faintheartedness, when she rejected their advances they backed off with surprising meekness.

The men she chased away were incessantly critical of her.

"When one of them starts to say nasty things about you, I know right away, aha, he's the latest one to try his luck!" Shizuko's voice was filled with high glee. The men forbade their wives to see Hiroko, and the wives, convinced their husbands would soon achieve social success, did as told. The only wife who went against her husband had the stuffing knocked out of her.

Shizuko, who was her boss's lover, had all the protection she needed to live in New York City, and she maintained a distance from the Japanese community.

"There's a little board marked 'closest spot to Spain in the USA.' It's stuck next to a clump of grass on a little cliff that hangs out over the ocean. Like it's praying that the grass will protect it from the wind off the waves. The closest house is fifteen minutes away by foot. I stand there looking out over the endless stretch of ocean, and I think, 'I've come really far. I can never go any farther than this.' And that thought makes me happy. Desperately happy."

When Charlie started to talk about the island where his band had spent a couple of summers working, the marijuana between his fingers turned to smoke, untouched.

"Nantucket was the base for the American whaling industry. At the beginning of the nineteenth century, a whaling ship from there fought with a white whale and sank. Based on the account of a man who'd been on that ship, Melville wrote *Moby-Dick*. You know about it, right? That's where the idea of Captain Ahab comes from."

The Japanese title was *Hakugei*, "White Whale." Captain Ahab, after losing his leg to the white whale, became obsessed with taking the creature's life. When she was a student, Hiroko remembered, she read the book with absorption, sensing that she had something in her life resembling Captain Ahab's white whale. Had her lifelong inner struggle with that something been in vain?

"I'd like to visit there," she said.

He put her hand to his lips. "When?" There was a shadow in his voice.

"After I put together enough money for the trip."

The proposition of selling the apartment had been rejected. The branch manager would not reveal whose decision it was.

Once again, Hiroko asked Shizuko to sell her jewels. Her mother had bought them for her when she was preparing to marry; she'd never worn them. There was a variety of them, jewels she had forgotten she even had. She couldn't estimate their worth, but one item still had the price tag attached: 1.8 million yen.

For once, there was a phone call from Sakiko. "You bounced a check, I hear!" The criticism in her tone was that of a moralistic suburban housewife, someone who goes around complaining how busy she is while actually having time on her hands. So what if she'd bounced a check? Hiroko said nothing.

"What did you use the money for?"

This time her tone was sharp, accusatory. She's getting to be more and more like Eiko, Hiroko thought.

"Paul's worried, too."

Paul. Yes, Hiroko vaguely remembered a man by that name.

"You never call, and when I do, your line is always busy. I have plenty of things to do. I can't spend all my time worrying about you."

Don't bother, please, Hiroko said silently. *I'm going to go on a trip somewhere far beyond your reach. A trip in a different dimension from a family outing.*

At the other end of the line, Hideto started to cry. "Oh, for heaven's sake!" The receiver slammed down.

Hiroko kept the receiver pressed to her ear. She wanted to stay connected, if only to the dial tone. *Sakiko sounded worried about me, but then as soon as her kid starts to cry, she hangs up. Everybody and their uncle puts family first. I have nothing. Nothing. I am a loser. A failure.*

7 Faraway Island

A solitary island rose out of the sea. The sun was setting, as if it were being pulled toward the bottom of a horizon banked in gray clouds. Hiroko had a sense of having come far.

They drove off the ferry, and where all the other cars turned left, Charlie steered their rental car to the right. He turned right again and pulled up in front of a white building trimmed for no apparent reason in glittering gold. A bellboy in a gold-braided uniform came bounding out and removed their luggage from the trunk: Hiroko's fine leather suitcases and cosmetics case—a three-piece set from Saks Fifth Avenue, ordered for a museum-prowling trip to Europe with Paul that had never come off—and Charlie's large duffel bag, which had about reached the end of its life.

The bellboy stared at the pair of them with a frank curiosity born of monotony—an Asian woman dressed in a smart Madison Avenue suit and a white man with a worn corduroy jacket slung around his shoulders: two people as ill-matched as their luggage. Watching him watch them, Hiroko felt again as if she had come to the back of beyond.

Charlie handled the reception desk exchange with aplomb, an indication that four-star hotels were nothing new to him. Probably from the time he was little his parents had brought him to places like this.

By the wide lawn facing the sea was a neat row of cottages, all alike. They were guided to one surrounded by shrubbery.

Under the bellboy's eyes, Charlie took out a couple of bills from the pocket of his jeans. Seeing a joint of marijuana stuck to one of them, Hiroko giggled, to her own surprise. Charlie carefully smoothed out the joint as if it were something precious and laid it on the table, where it attracted attention, if not an outright stare.

"This place is called The White Elephant," Charlie said when they were alone. "In English a white elephant is something burdensome, a costly encumbrance."

Suddenly, as if her name had been called, Hiroko cast her eyes down.

"Like me," said Charlie.

Raising her head at the sound of his muffled voice, she saw him standing there, his thin figure dull with sadness. For a time they remained unmoving, both of them gazing down, she seated and he standing, lost in their private thoughts.

She sensed him come abruptly to himself, pick up the marijuana on the table and head into the bathroom.

In contrast to the sumptuousness of the main building, the bedroom was simple in design, with walls of plain unvarnished wood. There were twin beds with covers of heavy, ivory-colored cotton. She sat down on one of them and opened a book. Reading was her salvation. From the world of white elephants— encumbrances—she entered Swann's world, *In Search of Lost Time.*

"What are ya reading?"

Suddenly, there was Charlie's clinging voice. Now stoned, he was standing at her side, jiggling. A meaningless array of words followed. As she remained silent, fixing him with provocative eyes, he turned and walked out of the room. Wondering at herself—for normally nothing could distract her from her reading—she tossed her book aside and went after him.

"I'm hungry," he said. "Room service, please," he added with his usual snort of laughter.

"What do you want?"

His only response was the typical, self-satisfied smile of someone stoned on marijuana. A vision of a hamburger the way he liked it came to her, making her shudder. When had she sunk to Sakiko's and Eiko's level? She picked up the phone and dialed room service.

Hiroko awoke when the morning sun struck her eyes through a crack in the curtains. This was why she disliked sleeping away from home. She'd gone to considerable pains to keep sunlight out of her bedroom in New York. The branch manager had given personal instructions to the carpenters to make sure all was done to her satisfaction.

Over in the next bed Charlie was asleep, rolled up in the bedspread, still dressed.

Her doctor had prescribed sleeping medication that he promised would be sufficiently strong, and once it took effect hardly anything could awaken her. Without it, she couldn't sleep. Not knowing how long they would stay, she had brought along a fair amount, but what if she ran out? Would a little island like this even have such a drug?

She stole out of bed, opened the door to the living room, and was assailed by the smell of marijuana and cigarettes. On the floor, amid fallen scraps of leftover hamburger and stubs from the overflowing ashtray there were several records and a portable record player. So that's what had been in his duffel bag.

She opened a window to air out the room. Though this act of solicitude on her part aroused a bit of self-scorn, she breathed in the sea breeze with relief. It would feel wonderful to be out on the beach, but she didn't have the nerve to go alone.

There was a knock at the door. As she was hesitating whether to answer, her ears caught the sound of someone inserting a key in the keyhole. The door swung open, and in stepped a maid. A young white woman in a pink uniform who automatically said, "I'm sorry," though her face plainly said, *Lady, if you're in here, say so!* Hiroko flinched, at a loss. Holding herself tightly in check so she wouldn't shake, she stammered that her companion was still asleep, with a glance at the bedroom.

The maid said she'd come back in the afternoon and started to leave. Then she gave Hiroko a dubious look and, after a moment's indecision, asked, "Are you really registered here? Did you check in and everything?"

"Yes."

Hiroko's throat was constricted; no other words came. The maid left with a jingle of keys, as if to say she would see about that. Hiroko had to report this incident to the manager: the realization came to her at the same time as the thought that it would be too much trouble. She quickly decided against doing anything troublesome—the family policy was deeply ingrained.

At the sound of the maid returning, Hiroko woke Charlie up. He tore from the bed to the bathroom. The living room was by then tidied, all trace of marijuana, in particular, carefully removed. Recalling what Sakiko had said about housework being good for the soul, Hiroko was convinced her sister's spiritual life must be barren.

Seated by the cottage entrance, to make up for time wasted

tidying the room she hungrily began reading Kafka's *The Castle*. As she read, the protagonist's struggle to convince the landlord and others that he had an invitation from the Count echoed the skepticism that she and Charlie had encountered from the maid.

"I won't clean the bathroom today."

At the sound of the maid's sharp-edged voice, Hiroko lifted her eyes and watched the pink uniform depart, bathed in soft sunshine. Beyond lay the real world.

Charlie came out in his bathrobe, sat down next to her and lit up a joint. One puff and he was cheerful and refreshed, as relaxed as if he were in his own home. He looked up with a radiant smile at the sky, where one thin cloud could be seen, and planted a kiss on Hiroko's cheek. They never kissed on the lips.

"Let's go to the beach," he said.

Hiroko sprang up, took out the things they would need from her suitcase, and transferred them to a soft leather bag— something else she'd bought for a trip with Paul. As far back as she could remember, when Eiko got ready to take their younger sisters out somewhere she always used to bustle around like this. Hiroko had always looked on with secret condescension, thinking what a little housewife her sister had turned into. A slightly bitter smile now crossed her face.

They bought food at a roadside grocery, beer and whiskey at a liquor store. Charlie, already high, kept on alternately pressing down on the accelerator and releasing it while giving her funny looks as if checking the identity of the woman beside him.

The large, white, New England-style houses lining the road were prim, letting foreigners know that they were not welcome. They gave way to fields, with here and there a low tree. Charlie drove down an unpaved lane and into a concrete parking lot. Before their eyes stretched the beach. He set straight off and Hiroko followed him, carrying everything.

When they stopped, the sight of the sun-caressed sea sank into her very marrow. There were no whys or wherefores. She had forgotten such scenery existed. Had she ever known? When Eiko used to take Fusako and Sakiko swimming, she would invite Hiroko along, but never once had Hiroko set aside her book to join them.

Along the right was a row of summer houses that seemed to declare ownership over the sand. Avoiding the public beach, which although deserted suggested the mess remaining after summer fun, they settled on the sand by the summer houses. Hiroko took a drag on the joint Charlie handed her, ate a bacon, lettuce, and tomato sandwich, and drank a beer.

Coming here had been the right thing to do. The sea breeze felt good, though she had expected to shiver. Gingerly, she stretched out on the mat that Charlie had picked up matter-of-factly at the grocery. How strange to look up at the sky. Who knew that blue sky and white clouds could have such intensity?

Charlie stared at the horizon, his brows furrowed and his mouth in a twist. What was he feeling and thinking? He didn't say and Hiroko didn't ask. They didn't communicate in words, yet she believed communication did take place between them.

Suddenly they heard a shrill shout. Hiroko, then Charlie, turned to look. A middle-aged blonde woman had come out on the terrace of the summer house they had assumed was closed and was waving her arms, ordering them to go away. They had partially encroached on the sand in front of her house.

"These people don't own the beach," said Charlie in a tone of deep malevolence. "But if she calls the police it could get ugly. My mother's the same damn way. Some people just love to call the police. And the police take their side, too."

They moved to the beach in front of the parking lot.

When the horizon began to turn purple in the lingering light, Charlie spoke up: "Brr, let's go." His voice sounded as if he'd just come back from somewhere.

He was too stoned to drive, so Hiroko took the wheel. Night came early on the tourist-empty island. Keeping one eye on Charlie bouncing around in the seat beside her, Hiroko watched out the window for a place to pick up something for supper. She felt herself becoming more and more like Eiko. By the side of the road was a Chinese takeout place, the kind you might come across anywhere in the world. A Chinese woman with an air of strength, as of roots planted deep in the earth, looked in the direction Hiroko pointed and understood what she wanted without the need for words. The thought that language served no purpose was depressing. Hiroko was momentarily relieved to encounter a fellow Asian on this all-too-Caucasian island, a sentimental whim at once surprising and disillusioning.

When she returned to the car carrying white paper cartons filled with fried rice and sweet-and-sour pork, Charlie was curled up like a puppy, fast asleep. She deplored what she had become, a person who did things like this to avoid the cost of room service.

The white building rose up in the gloom. A white elephant was an encumbrance, something that cost money. *Me*, thought Hiroko.

In the afternoons, chased out by the maid, they would leave the hotel and explore the beach, staying until it was dark out and they couldn't stand the cold. Days of marijuana and cigarettes, beer and sandwiches. A week went by. They each grew concerned about their dwindling supply, Charlie's of marijuana, hers of sleeping pills.

On Nantucket, this small island in the Atlantic Ocean, half an hour's drive north, west, or south from the ferry landing took you straight to the sea. The name "Nantucket" was an Indian word meaning "faraway island."

Hiroko spent less time thinking. Gradually she was freed of the pressure to think that she'd felt ever since childhood, to think or else have her existence negated. When Charlie lightly laid his hand on her, or when he snorted with laughter, she felt strangely fulfilled. Laughter concealed unfathomable darkness. She could cry whenever she felt like it now, so why didn't she? Charlie did nothing, and she asked nothing of him. Only now did she see that it was possible to spend time together in this way.

The hotel presented them with a week's bill.

She paid the bill and went back to their cottage. As she checked the contents of her cash envelope, her spirits sank. The disappearing money caused her energy to disappear, too. Everything was too much trouble. Nothing seemed to matter.

When Shizuko had handed her the cash from the sale of her jewels, despite her ignorance of the value of such things, Hiroko had been amazed at how little it was. "This is all?" she'd blurted out.

"The jewels were in bad condition," explained Shizuko. "Damaged, every single one. Under the circumstances, what could you expect? Not that you'd understand. You may have more brains than you know what to do with, Hiroko, but you know zilch about the real world."

When she'd reported this exchange to Charlie, for once he got angry. "She took advantage of your weakness," he fumed. At one time Hiroko would have been furious to be told such a thing, but now she thought it over calmly, wondering what her weakness might be.

"What exactly is my weakness?"

"Loneliness, for one. Pride for another."

Rebellion and recognition welled up in her simultaneously. She knew it was true but didn't care to admit it. Charlie went on:

"Loneliness is nothing unusual. But yours is fundamental and pathological. There must have been something wrong in the way you were brought up. Being unwanted at birth leaves a scar that lasts a lifetime." He rolled a joint, lit it, and took a drag before continuing. "The reason I'm addicted to grass and booze has to do with not being wanted as a baby."

She took the marijuana from his hand and pulled deeply on it. As she beat on her chest to rid herself of pent-up feelings, he helped by pounding her on the back.

"It was Shizuko who got the band members to go to you for checks," he said.

People took action based on Hiroko's money. They approached her because she had money. All her life she had coped with this fact, yet now her mind was in turmoil. She felt desolate.

Maybe she should go back to Japan. No, she couldn't do that. Her pride wouldn't allow it. She trembled to think what her father, Morimasa, would say. Returning home was definitely not an option.

I wasn't a boy, but everyone in the family had high expectations of me, just the same as if I were the eldest son. I have to go back as a famous and successful artist, prove my life choices were right. I always said I'd return home covered in glory—"decorated in brocade." The very expression is saturated with Japanese sentiment, the sort of thing an immigrant would say. What made that come to me? Last night while I was eating my pork chop, I remember I had a sudden urge for a bowl of ochazuke, *rice and green tea. I always hated* ochazuke, *it was such a sorry excuse for a meal…*

Glancing up at the bright afternoon sky with sleep-lidded eyes, Charlie said, "Let's go sailing." It sounded as if he were trying to shake off a bad dream.

They arrived at the harbor armed with their usual stockpile of beer and sandwiches. Charlie chatted with a fellow renting boats and picked out one of the sailboats moored at the pier. While it was being readied, he took a deep breath, went over to the public phone, and placed a collect call. When someone came on the line, he started to speak in the polite tones of a prep school boy. "Yes, Mother." Listening with an eye on the worn leather shoes that seemed to tell the story of his life, Hiroko had no doubt he was indeed talking to his mother.

The rental guy came. Seeming to sense the serious nature of the phone conversation, he signaled wordlessly to Hiroko that all was ready. Before long Charlie hung up. He looked out at the horizon with the cheerless expression of a student just issued a failing grade. Hiroko handed him a cup of coffee she'd brought from the boathouse. "Thank you," he said, looking at her with eyes of a blackness so deep she felt a chill.

Charlie got in the boat first, then held out a hand and helped Hiroko, her figure bulky with extra layers of clothing, to hop aboard. He lifted the sail and took the tiller. He'd grown up in a family that went in for marine sports. Hiroko pictured him as a boy, learning the art of sailing from his father with his mother standing off at one side, martini glass in hand. Then she saw black smoke emanate from the father and mother and envelop the young Charlie.

They sailed out to sea. The sea was calm, with here and there a cloud in the sky. The sunlight felt warm, but Hiroko was afraid to shed any of her extra layers. They somehow protected her from a creeping sense of anxiety and dread. When she was happy, she entertained feelings of guilt. *I don't deserve to be happy; I failed at everything, disappointed my father, lost my sisters' respect. I'm a loser,* she whispered to herself in Japanese.

Barefoot and wearing only a sweatshirt, no jacket, Charlie worked the sail. He looked around with a faint smile, the darkness in his eyes now nearly gone. His shoulder-length hair blew in the wind, and his expression turned suddenly melancholy.

Bathed in soft sunlight, the sea gently rocked their boat. Hiroko was a virtual stranger to the ocean. In the summer when her sisters used to rent a seaside house and take off, she alone would stay in Tokyo and study. Their father, Morimasa, used to praise her for that, making her happy and proud. One other time, he praised her. It happened during wartime.

As a schoolgirl, Hiroko was mobilized along with other students to work in an outlying area manufacturing airplanes. In a bleak place far from the sea, where clouds of dust filled the air, she slept in a tiny hut with her classmates, perennially hungry and hemmed in by rules.

"Japan is sure to win. Whatever happens, in the end a divine wind will blow and set things right." People believed this—a way of thinking that Hiroko privately looked down on as irrational and sentimental. But her father also said that Japan would definitely win, and she had faith in him. If she'd been a boy, she could have become a member of the kamikaze special attack unit and made him proud. Deep down she was full of regret that she'd been born female.

Yet she wavered between what she thought about the war and what her father said about it; deplored herself for doing so; felt apologetic for doubting him.

Day after day there were air raids, but that day there were none. The quiet felt strange. Sensing that the United States had by then seized the initiative in the war, Hiroko was just wondering if today was an American holiday, or perhaps a day when the Americans had decreed there would be no fighting, when everyone was ordered to gather by the radio.

A hard-to-understand voice issued from the set, mixed with static. Everyone else paid close attention, but Hiroko, fearful that enemy airplanes might suddenly appear overhead again, kept looking nervously up at the sky. The factory man who would normally have lashed out angrily at her was busy wiping tears from his eyes. When the broadcast ended, the director spoke to them and she learned that the war was over.

We lost, didn't we? Then why not come out and say so? Why just say "it's over"? Japan made itself a laughingstock, fighting a war with planes made by girls. All the thoughts she'd been holding back came rushing up, sticking in her throat. The factory man was now sobbing aloud. The other adults around her were crestfallen and utterly changed. She was not afraid of them.

When Hiroko went back to Tokyo, her father praised her for having devoted herself to her country to the bitter end, elevating what she had considered a complete waste of time into a precious experience.

The house where they formerly lived had burned down in an air raid, so they all lived together in a little rented house, she and her father and her mother and sisters, now back from evacuation.

Japan's defeat in a war her father had predicted they would win made her faith in him waver. She blamed herself for being a bad daughter. She felt lost, uncertain what to believe.

School began, and Hiroko was amazed to see the change that had come over her teachers. No more sermons, not even any complaints. They seemed to find daily life a struggle and cozied up to the children of tradesmen with ample access to food.

In the grade one year below Hiroko was a spunky girl said to be the leader of the bad kids. One day, something important that she'd brought to sewing class disappeared—the sleeve of a haori, a short coat to wear over kimono, that her mother prized. Back then, all sorts of things used to get stolen, from lunchboxes to shoes. When the girl insisted that the teacher examine everyone's belongings to search for her missing property, Hiroko was thunderstruck. Even more amazingly, the teacher could not refuse and actually did as asked. None of this would have been thinkable prior to the defeat. Hiroko told herself that what she needed was that girl's spunk and dynamism. Yet when she did run into the girl, envy made Hiroko lower her head and creep away.

Next the girl declared that clothes inspections were stupid and boycotted them. At first she was joined by several supporters, but as the teachers calmly remonstrated with them, one by one the others yielded, leaving only her and one other holdout. In the end, the principal came and, unbelievably, bowed his head and requested them to submit to the inspections. They did not.

Everyone assumed they would be expelled, but they weren't. Hiroko shuddered, knowing that the last remaining authority had crumbled.

She too thought the clothes inspection was stupid and wondered privately how long they intended to keep it up. However, she made sure no one suspected how she felt. Had she been in the same grade as the rebellious girl, she would never have joined forces with her. Her father would have been furious. Fear of the wrathful paternal gaze and daunting paternal voice that obliterated her existence were what kept Hiroko showing up faithfully for inspection.

Among her classmates, most of whom thought only of becoming "good wives and wise mothers," there was nobody Hiroko wanted for a friend. She would have liked to get to know that girl in the grade below, whom people apparently now shunned, but she lacked the courage to say hi. Compared to her, the other girl had an intimidating depth of knowledge and power of thought, and was capable of taking action, too. Above all, she was brimming with confidence. Dazzling self-confidence—something Hiroko would never have. Suppose she did work up her nerve and talk to the other girl, and the other girl turned out to be her superior in every respect—what would that do to Hiroko's pride?

The year Japan lost the war, Hiroko had been in the fifth year of a girls' higher school; the year following, she entered high school under the revised system as a third-year student, eventually moving on to the English department of a women's college. She believed that she was allowed to do so for two reasons: first, because people's thinking about women changed after the war, as seen in the acceptance of women's suffrage; second, because her father was wrapped up in business affairs with no attention to spare for his family. In the English department she studied the English language and was struck by its logicality and clarity of expression. All things Japanese became increasingly repugnant to her.

With securing a food supply no longer a problem, her mother, Sadako, began devoting herself to obtaining American products through a dry cleaner with ties to the PX at the US military base. Sadako smoked American cigarettes, used nail polish, lipstick and other cosmetics, and went out dancing.

Seeing Hiroko at her books, her mother would caution, "Don't strain your eyes, now. It would be terrible if you ruined your eyesight and had to wear glasses. Nobody wants to marry a woman with glasses." Under her breath, Hiroko would reply, *I'm not getting married. That's the last thing I'd ever want to do—get married and lead a silly life like yours.*

After the defeat, adults did a complete turnabout. Black became white. Never again would Hiroko trust her own country. The war had stolen a crucial time in her life, when she was on the cusp of adulthood. She'd lost something fundamental as a human being. Her utter lack of desire to return to Japan wasn't solely a matter of pride.

Hiroko went back and forth in her mind. There was no place for her in the States, either. Where should she go? And now her money was gone.

She held herself stiffly, seated on the edge of the boat. In the distance was the vague outline of the island. The sail flapped in the wind. Charlie was sitting in the bottom of the boat, lost in his own world, looking up at the sail and smoking remnants of marijuana joints he'd scraped together. She felt suffocated, desolate.

She turned her head and looked at the sunlight sparkling on the dark blue water. Shafts of sunlight trying to penetrate the surface were turned away by the darkness below. All at once she felt her heart freeze, and a shiver ran down her spine. The shiver entered her hands, which separated from the edge of the boat. Her body leaned backward. Something in the core of her body, of her spirit, gave way and she fell toward the water. She tried to catch onto the edge of the boat, or did she? A white elephant floated idly under the blue sky, of its giant frame only the head showing, and then vanishing.

Charlie shouted. But no, Hiroko couldn't be certain of that, either. She only wished it. Wished that he would cry out in concern. One shout, that was all she asked.

169

8 Avoid Trouble

Sakiko wondered if her sister Hiroko hadn't clung to the man called Charlie when he jumped in to save her—clung with all her might. That was what she had wanted: to cast aside her pride and just cling. And so they both had drowned.

Word of Hiroko's death arrived by way of Japan. When Paul realized that Morimasa wanted Sakiko to fly off and handle things, he had volunteered to go instead, taking the first available flight.

And handle things he had done—including consulting with Morimasa over the phone about cremating the body and scattering the ashes at sea, a prospect that had made Sakiko feel faint. Through an interpreter, Morimasa replied, "If that's what she wanted, do it." His response was instant, Paul said.

Sakiko, too, had heard Hiroko say she wanted her ashes scattered: "I don't want to be buried in Japan. Scatter my ashes at sea, someplace where the family won't know."

Hiroko had said this one night in LA after a dinner of Sakiko's spare ribs, toying with the leftover bones, her fingers smeared with sauce. Sakiko had been glad Hideto was still too young to understand. At the time Paul had laughed hard, as if she'd said something heart-stoppingly funny. But it was good he had remembered.

Eiko, when she heard that Paul had gone to New York, said over the phone, "Oh good! He's the best one to go, after all." The relief in her voice was unmistakable. Perhaps she sensed this was inappropriate, for she tacked on a long, rambling spiel of seemingly deliberate vagueness. Even giving her words the most favorable interpretation possible, Sakiko could only take them to mean, "Really we ought to go, but we probably couldn't get visas, so that's that."

Knowing Sakiko was unable to contradict her, Eiko hid her feelings in a flow of words, as if wrapping them in floss silk. A trick of evasion passed down by their mother, Sadako—one that Hiroko had hated.

Coming off the plane, Paul looked haggard. As he lifted Hideto in the air, his eyes were hollow. He even forgot to kiss Sakiko hello. Normally afraid of her driving, he slid into the passenger seat and shut his eyes.

When they got home, he showered, dove into bed, and was soon snoring. When dinner was ready, Hideto went over and woke his father by pinching his nose. Paul took his place at the dinner table, but he seemed uncertain where he was.

"Daddy, Daddy!"

Hideto's voice chimed relentlessly, and finally Paul seemed to grow aware of his wife and son. He listened to Hideto and made appropriate responses, though his manner was woefully mechanical. Days passed, and he gradually returned to normal and began to talk.

The branch manager had taken charge of cleaning out Hiroko's apartment. Her paintings were not well preserved, and he had asked Paul whether they were worth the cost of shipping them to Japan.

"'Things that have no value to you are the things we value most,' I told him, and he said if I wasn't the boss's son-in-law he'd paste me one—gave me a furious look, like this."

Hideto cowered at the face Paul made, and clung to Sakiko.

"I don't know if he was mad because he understood what I said, or because he didn't." Paul picked up Hideto and rubbed cheeks with him. "Sorry little buddy, didn't mean to scare you."

In the end a word from Morimasa had settled the matter, and the paintings were all shipped off. Learning that her father respected Hiroko's creative work came as a revelation to Sakiko. He was not simply someone to fear, then. She sensed that her dream of having a long heart-to-heart talk with him might one day come true.

In Hiroko's apartment, there were half-full glasses of wine and moldy scraps of bread and cheese left out on the table; spoiled milk, eggs, and fruit in the refrigerator; a load of dirty dishes in the dishwasher and one of dirty clothes in the washing machine. It looked like she only planned to be away a few days, Paul said. According to the branch manager, her bank account balance was ten dollars.

In the hotel room where the two of them had stayed, there were two hundred dollars hidden in a drawerful of underwear, and a little over a hundred dollars in the bag left on the boat. Those were Hiroko's total assets.

"There's supposed to be some jewelry Mother bought for her," said Sakiko. "Eiko's quite worried about it."

"Jewelry?" Paul echoed. When she nodded, he stared at her aghast and then declared, "You sisters are unbelievable. How could anyone be worried about jewelry at a time like this?"

Sakiko, too, thought there was something odd about the way, on learning of her sister's death, Eiko had mentioned the jewelry first off. But following long years of habit, she'd followed her sister's lead. She now followed Paul's lead, only thinking her sister had acted strangely because he had said so. Thinking for herself, making up her own mind—this was still beyond her.

He told her there'd been piles of marijuana butts everywhere in Hiroko's apartment. Since the hotel room had been cleaned, he couldn't say for sure, but the air there had smelled of reefer, too. "It all turned to smoke. So what?" He made it sound as if it didn't matter in the slightest.

Looking at her husband's gaunt appearance, Sakiko realized that the trip had exhausted him physically and mentally. She could have left Hideto with Ryoko and gone herself. *You're no different from your sisters,* she told herself in contrition. *You saw cleaning up after your sister's death as an inconvenience, and when Paul volunteered to go, you were relieved.*

Back in grade school, Sakiko's habit of stopping at the movie theater or the fruit parlor on her way home had escalated until she was skipping school entirely and spending the whole day at such places. The teacher found out and called her mother in for a conference. Sakiko had paid for her outings with money stolen from her father's wallet.

After the conference, her mother acted no different than usual. Silent and impassive, she boarded the train with Sakiko and got off with her at Sukiyabashi, the end of the line. She walked briskly along, much as if she were alone on a shopping trip in the backstreets of Ginza, and went into a Western-style restaurant, a favorite haunt of hers by the way the staff reacted. As the waitress set glasses of water on the table, she hurriedly ordered fried prawns and beer for herself, a hamburger steak and a cream soda for Sakiko, all the while fumbling in her purse for cigarettes. Finally, from between the gold clasps of the alligator-leather purse she'd bought at Ameyoko, the black market for American products in Okachimachi, she pulled out a pack, lit one, and blew the smoke out of her nostrils. After one more puff her face began showing signs of oblivion, and by the time she finished her beer, she appeared to have forgotten all unpleasantness.

She never so much as glanced at Sakiko. Motioning to the hamburger with her chin, eyes elsewhere, she said, "Eat it while it's hot." Those were the only words she spoke that day. She wasn't angry. This was how she always was.

Eiko and Fusako knew their mother had been summoned to school, but neither of them could ask what for. Even if they had wanted to, she was gone so much of the time they never had the opportunity. Eiko, who had taken charge of the family, finally broke down and asked Sakiko, but Sakiko was afraid of a scolding and so she pretended not to know. In the end it was as if nothing had ever happened.

As she became an adolescent, Sakiko began to spend nights away from home. One of the young maids got worried and informed her mother, but all she did was stare suspiciously at the girl. Eiko, by then married and living elsewhere, never heard anything about it.

Once a boy whom Sakiko had been seeing but whom she had started to avoid came barging into the house in search of her. He yelled and grabbed her by the arm, trying to take her away. Her mother, whose advancing age now kept her home much more often, stayed in her room with the door shut. Even if the boy had charged into her room, she would probably only have given him a careless glance, treating him so curtly that he'd have been brought up short. Fusako had been out. What would she have done if she'd been there, Sakiko wondered as she grappled with the boy. Probably leaned against the pillar in the entryway and said with a smirk, "Take her, she's all yours. Thanks a lot!"

The maid had called the police. By the time they arrived, her mother was gone.

When Sakiko returned home after talking to the police, her mother was giving instructions for dinner quite as usual. Glancing at Sakiko, who was trembling with a welter of emotions, she said, "Oh, you're back," as if nothing had happened.

Even at dinner, her mother ate silently as usual. She was not angry. She simply didn't want to face the problem squarely. She herself had been raised in such an environment, and so it became the rule for the Morimoto women to tiptoe around trouble.

One thing she said went through Sakiko like a nail in the heart: "Don't tell your father. He'd get angry at me."

"Charlie was a reefer addict with designs on Hiroko's money. I mean, he was a jazz musician, wasn't he? That says it all. No doubt about it."

After Sakiko made this declaration, Paul shook his head and asked her to refrain from judging people by what they did for a living. Ordinarily he would have scolded her in strong terms, looking her straight in the eye, but instead his gaze was slightly off center, grazing her ear.

"What were Charlie's parents like? How did they act?" She was curious, but he wouldn't say. Normally he would have drawn upon his excellent powers of observation to tell some wickedly funny anecdote.

He made time to go to the beach. "Take Hideto with you," Sakiko begged, but he made a gesture that meant *Right now I can't* and set off alone.

"I saw him staring off at the horizon," a friend of hers told her. "I hesitated to speak to him." Sakiko was touched at how grieved Paul was by her sister's death.

He had spent quite a while in New York, overseeing the wrapping of Hiroko's paintings and whatnot, and at Morimasa's instructions the branch manager sent a check to cover his expenses. Paul tore it up without a word. Since he was usually a stickler about money, this seemed out of character for him, and Sakiko pressed him for an explanation. All he would say was "No one was ever as unhappy as her," which explained nothing. Unable to tell whether his rigid body might collapse or whether he might suddenly turn on her, Sakiko decided not to pursue the matter.

He painted a work titled *Hiroko*. Sakiko thought she could make out in it Hiroko's intelligence, pride, arrogance, loneliness, and confusion, but lacking confidence, she checked with a friend who had known her sister. The friend concurred with her impression, and commented, "He really observed her in depth." Sakiko rejoiced to think that despite all the fascinating people around him, Paul had taken the trouble to make a close study of Hiroko.

By Christmas, Paul was back to his usual free and easy self. The family spent the holiday skiing in Aspen. Hideto was excited by his first-ever experience of snow; he and Paul made a great big snowman, with red apples for eyes. Sakiko, used to seeing charcoal for eyes, found the red-eyed snowman rather disconcerting, but for Hideto, red eyes for snowmen would now be the norm. People grew up in different environments and so they came to follow different customs and have different ways of thinking.

When they got home, there was a bulky package from Fusako. Too big to fit in the mailbox, it was sitting in front of the door. Sakiko was always glad for a package from Japan, but especially so after spending several days in the exclusive company of whites. As she took Hideto to the bathroom, watching over him as he peed, washed his hands, and gargled, her heart fluttered with anticipation. She opened the firmly sealed bag and found notebook-sized Xerox copies, quite a few. There was a card from Fusako that said only, "Thought you'd be interested." She scanned the papers. The handwriting was Hiroko's. Sakiko's heart leapt.

Hideto came over to say something to her, and she left the bundle of papers on a side table. Paul, bringing things in from the car, deposited on top of it the bag of groceries they'd picked up on the way home from the airport. Sakiko told him what was on the bottom. He said only, "Huh," with little apparent interest, and went back to the car. Had he no more feeling than that for her sister? If you weren't a blood relation you got over your grief awfully fast, she thought with a chill.

As she bustled around unpacking and getting supper on, the papers stayed on her mind. Reading anything at all in Japanese was pleasurable, but this was some seemingly important record that her sister Hiroko had left behind, piquing her interest all the more. The closely-written lines called out to her.

After she'd put Hideto to bed and Paul had gone off to his studio, she flew to the side table. The papers were gone.

They'd been there before when she put the groceries away. What had Paul done with them? She called the person who lived next door to the studio—the number she had been given for emergencies. Fearfully, she asked for Paul.

"Hello." Out of sorts from the first, Paul brushed off her question with a gruff "I don't know." Had he seen it when he left the house, she asked, and he answered irritably in the negative.

She searched the house and went through the trash. In the morning she woke Hideto early and asked him, then searched the house again, but didn't find it.

Sakiko phoned Fusako, explained the situation, and asked her to send another copy. Fusako listened to her account with strange calmness, occasionally chiming in: "I see. Vanished into thin air, huh." She agreed to send another copy. Sakiko had fully expected her sister to blame her for being so careless, laugh scornfully, and declare that making another copy was too damn much trouble. Having received assurance that a replacement would soon be on the way, she did not have the energy to ask about the contents.

One page was enough. It came as a punch in the gut. She froze bodily, from her blood to her heart to her soul. So that was how it had been. She'd known about the other women in his life, but her own sister Hiroko...

Paul had hurried off to New York in order to hide the evidence. The one thing he couldn't read because it was written in Japanese had been shipped off to Japan with Hiroko's other effects, where it drew Fusako's attention. *Fusako hates me with a passion,* Sakiko thought. She was struck by the darkness in her sister's heart.

Sakiko phoned Eiko.

"Fusako did that?" Eiko was rendered speechless. Silence followed.

"Did you know?"

After some hesitation, Eiko said, "I read it. But I can't believe Fusako would send it to you..."

Sakiko let loose her anger and resentment toward Fusako. The subject of the relations between Hiroko and Paul was too raw, too awkward for either her or Eiko to bring up. Or were they only following the Morimoto family policy of skirting around any difficulty?

After Sakiko had complained and wept, she paused in

exhaustion. "Feel better?" said Eiko. "Long distance calls are expensive, so I'm hanging up."

And just like that, so casually that Sakiko was taken aback, Eiko hung up.

9 Saying No

The painting *Hiroko* that he had painted disappeared from the wall where it used to hang, just inside the entryway, but Paul said nothing. Neither did Sakiko. This although every time they opened the front door, like it or not their eyes went straight to that spot. That was why she'd chosen to hang the painting there in the first place. Until she found out the nasty truth that clung to her like a shadow and gave her no rest, picked up the painting using the same rubber gloves she used to clean the toilet with, and tossed it into a big garbage can, Paul and she used to pause in front of it daily. What he may have been thinking she didn't know and didn't care to know, but she had always prayed for her sister's happiness in heaven. She herself was in hell…

Days went by as if nothing had happened. The one difference was that the name "Hiroko" never crossed their lips. Not even Hideto said it. Now eleven, he sensed that something alarming had happened between his parents, and that they were pretending otherwise. When the three of them were together, they outdid each other in talking to him. He was baffled.

One night when he sat down for dinner, Hideto took his fork and spoon in hand and started tapping his plate and cup the way he used to do when he was little, lightly at first, then gradually more rhythmically. Watching him show off like a jazz drummer, Sakiko remembered the time she and Hiroko had gone to the jazz club in New York to hear John Coltrane.

Without her meaning for it to happen, her hand shot out and grabbed his hand holding the fork, squeezing hard. Normally she never did this sort of thing. And normally Hideto would have yelled "Ow! Mommy, you're hurting me!" and pulled away, glaring, but he did not. He held still and didn't say a word.

Suddenly he started to cry. Without moving the hand she held fast, he laid the spoon on the table and wiped his tears with his other hand.

She put her arms around him. "Sorry." Tears started in her eyes, too.

Another time, sitting at the table, Hideo reached out for anything in arm's length, put it in his mouth, then tossed it aside, the way infants do. Then he would stick something else in his mouth and do the same thing all over again. The way he watched for his parents' reaction, though, was not at all babylike.

"Stop it, Hideto!" Paul scolded.

Hideto gave him an upturned glance and said, "I want to know what they are, Daddy." He stuck a thumb in his mouth.

"Quit horsing around," said Paul, his tone slightly harsher. He probably wanted to explode, thought Sakiko, but couldn't let out his anger on someone so vulnerable. She smiled to herself.

"I'm not horsing. I really don't know what's going on in this house. I'm just trying to find out." Hideto sounded as if he had returned to his eleven-year-old self, or perhaps not.

It wouldn't do to let Hideto be affected, Sakiko told herself, and locked the sordid mess away in her heart. Of course she couldn't tell her son outright "Daddy and Aunt Hiroko were having an affair," but even when she was alone with Paul, she didn't broach the topic. Often when she thought Hideto was in his room, she would find him hiding behind the sofa or crouched behind a door, so she couldn't let down her guard. He seemed to have regressed to early childhood. Her heart and mind were full to bursting with the truth she had stumbled on; containment was painful, but for Hideto's sake she bit her tongue and said nothing. At the same time, she took to scolding her son hysterically over nothing. His presence grated on her nerves.

She never realized that she, too, had become a victim of the Morimoto rule for women: avoid unpleasantness.

A letter came from Eiko.

Father said the strangest thing: "I was wrong to keep send-ing Hiroko money without making any effort to find out what she was doing."

She died in an accident, but he seems to think she committed suicide. That's impossible. I can't imagine where he ever got such an idea. She was the finest of us four. She would never have done such a thing. She was a successful New York art-ist, wasn't she, Sakiko? Besides, she would have known that doing a thing like that would disgrace the family.

But Father's instincts are sharp, so I am uneasy. I realize there is no point in telling you any of this when you are living such a pleasant, carefree life over there, but Fusako won't listen to me...

We have the children's futures to think of. What would happen if talk of suicide started to spread? They have to find jobs and marriage partners—proper Japanese ones, too. One person in the family married to a foreigner is enough. To tell you the truth, it's an inconvenience.

Sakiko, after you read this letter, tear it in little pieces and throw it away. No one's eyes but yours must ever see it. Understand?

Sakiko started to laugh at the last line—after all, the letter was written in Japanese, and she lived in an all-white community— but then her face stiffened, and tears came.

What difference did it make if it was an accident or suicide? All she knew was that she had no desire ever to see or hear Hiroko's name again. She crumpled Eiko's fine white stationery into a ball and flung it into the garbage can, as if it were Hiroko herself.

Relieved, she glanced at Paul, who complained constantly these days of being "too busy." Unlike before, she felt no desire to have him around the house. Merely sensing his presence was enough to depress her. "I'll sleep in my studio," he would say, and as she never responded, he took to staying there without bothering to tell her. On the occasional nights when he slept at home, rather than have one of them sleep in the guest room (this Hideto would have found odd), they lay awkwardly on opposite edges of the double bed and tried to ignore each other's presence. They avoided meeting each other's eyes. When they had something to tell or hand each other, they did so with eyes averted.

Sakiko's heart was like a paved street deflecting fierce rays of the sun.

"Mommy, stay till I fall asleep." Hideto turned anxious eyes on her. Ever since the discovery she'd made, he had been this way.

"Don't worry, I'm right here," she answered, her mind elsewhere. So he wouldn't realize how impatient she was for him to fall asleep, she rested her hand on his covers, willing it not to twitch—but her fingers drummed of their own accord. She started to jump up, and he cried out, "Don't go!"

Damn it all! Until now he'd been so good about saying "Goodnight, Mommy," and putting himself to bed. She gritted her teeth and waited, and when release finally came, she took a bottle of wine and a glass into the bedroom. After one sip, the door opened and in stepped Paul.

"I'm living with a ghost. A ghost who wastes away by the day. Paintings disappear from walls…this is a regular haunted house."

The next moment, wine bottle and glass were in his hands, and their contents were being dumped in the toilet. Sakiko ran to shut the half-open door, praying that Hideto wouldn't wake up.

"Are you ready to talk?" said Paul.

She flew toward the bathroom and reached for the doorknob. He swept her hand away and barred the door.

"If we go on like this, we're only going to wear each other out. You're already addicted to sleeping pills, and you're this close to being an alcoholic."

Maybe you're right about the sleeping pills, Hiroko replied silently, *but you're dead wrong about me being an alcoholic. I only drink after the sun starts to go down, and drinking isn't what's destroying my life. As you very well know.*

"You say you can't talk about things since you grew up in a

family that never communicated, but that just won't do. You're my wife and Hideto's mother. It's high time you grew up. I won't get angry, so there's nothing to be afraid of. Let's have a calm talk."

A calm talk? He must be joking. She wanted to rampage and yell. But she couldn't, because Hideto would hear. Her muscles stiffened. Every time Paul spoke in his carefully modulated tones, she got more wound up, till finally she blacked out.

Hideto's school called her in for a conference. His teacher looked startled at Sakiko's emaciated appearance and turned her dark brown eyes out the window, where a ray of sun was poking through the clouds. As if she'd found there the words she needed, she turned back to Sakiko, looked at her intently, and asked, "Has there been a problem at home of any kind?"

"My sister died in an accident," Sakiko said, with emphasis on the word "accident."

The teacher spoke words of condolence that were a balm to Sakiko's spirit, adding, "I asked Hideto if anything had happened, and even though it was something of this magnitude, he didn't tell me." She sounded as if her pride as a member of the teaching profession had been wounded.

"Hideto is behaving strangely," the teacher went on. "He tells lies, he hides his friends' belongings, he bangs on his desk suddenly in the middle of a lesson, he clams up and won't talk.... I think we can sum up his behavior in one phrase: infantile regression. This often happens when there is a problem at home. Does anything else come to mind?"

After having the effect on Hideto pointed out to her, Sakiko's maternal feelings stirred. Noticing some sort of internal shift in her, the teacher continued:

"Your sister's death came as a terrible blow to you. That's

entirely understandable, but at the same time, mark my words: if you don't give Hideto your full attention now, you'll regret it later. Any emotional damage he suffers now—trauma, we call it—will very likely afflict him down the road. Whether he is aware of it or not. This could determine the course of his entire life. I don't mean to alarm you, but we do need to pay more attention to the psychological effect of events that happen while people are growing up. The human mind is surprisingly complex."

The teacher spoke slowly and clearly, so Sakiko was able to follow what she said, nodding as she looked into her eyes. The teacher's gaze was mild and soft, yet there was apprehension in it as well. Yes, like the look in Mii-chan's mother's eyes long ago.

Sakiko wanted Hideto to be happy. That was why she had hidden away the horrible discovery that was eating her alive, why she had devoted so much effort to hiding it that it was driving her crazy—because she didn't want to hurt Hideto by getting into a fight with Paul.

She took a breath and looked again at the teacher, whose dark brown eyes were full of sincere concern for Hideto. At the same time, her eyes were telling Sakiko she must not run away

"Then are you saying I should talk to Hideto about the blow I suffered from my sister's death?"

"Your blow?" The teacher frowned, but quickly said in a quietly admonishing tone, "Do it while imagining you are Hideto. Try to enter into his thoughts and feelings." As if to underline how important this was, she looked firmly at Sakiko. "Tell him how you feel, what you think, and explain that that's what has changed you. Tell him, 'Mommy is sad. Mommy hasn't been herself lately, has she? This is why.' Speak calmly and clearly so he can understand. It's important that you look at things from his perspective. Never forget that. It's not easy to share feelings with someone, and for you it will be that much harder since English is not your native language. But you mustn't evade the problem. The worst thing you could do would be to run away from it."

Her words sank into Sakiko's heart.

It was true. In order to keep Hideto from knowing about her mixed-up feelings, she had shut off all avenues of communication with him. Avenues that should be shut and those that should not be, alike. The affair between Hiroko and Paul must be kept from him; that secret was necessary. But her feelings of loss and sorrow after her sister's death—those she could share with Hideto. That avenue needed to be kept open.

Sakiko couldn't tell Hideto right away. The teacher had advised her to sit down and talk things out with Paul first. Talk things out—yes, that's what she must do! Fortunately, that day Paul did not come home. If he had, then she might have made some thoughtless, impulsive remark the moment he walked in the door. He would have made some comeback and, no matter what he said, she would have responded with fear. Overwhelmed, her emotions would have gotten away from her, so that she ended up losing control and exploding. She was grateful that he didn't come home. But soon, she told herself. Soon she and Paul would talk. Sakiko needed to be able to talk to her son.

She went to his room. He was sleeping with his thumb in his mouth, like a toddler. His face was twisted, and he was groaning. He must be having a nightmare. Maybe she should shake him awake, the way the maids used to do with her when she was little. But however gentle they tried to be, when she woke up the faces she saw were always filled with irritation. If she wakened Hideto now, he might see the same look on her face—the thought terrified her.

Sunlight relentlessly filled every corner of the house again that day. Ryoko sliced the dark, adzuki bean jelly, she had brought from Japan. "When I have it in Japan I always think *yokan* is delicious," she commented, "but not so much when I have it here. Maybe it's all this sunshine. Let's make the room a little darker." They drew the curtains.

Sakiko remembered that somewhere around the house was a copy of Tanizaki Jun'ichiro's *In Praise of Shadows,* one that Hiroko had avidly read on her visit while muttering about how sick she was of the everlasting brightness.

The next moment it all came spilling out. Sakiko found herself talking as if a dam had burst.

Paul and Hiroko's betrayal.

Tea and *yokan* forgotten, Ryoko listened with a grim expression, mouth twisted in a frown. She wore no makeup, and her heavy eyebrows twitched.

Fusako's cruelty in sending the diary.

Sakiko had gone all the way back to the abuse she suffered as a child before the furious stream of words began to soften, like a runaway horse gradually calming down. Seeing Ryoko's skeptical expression, she said, "I've started to feel like I understand a little how Fusako feels. I still need time, though." Ryoko looked still more skeptical, and shook her head.

As she described her feelings toward Fusako and Hideto, and Hideto's infantile regression, Sakiko's heart ached and buzzed with uncertainty. What to do? She longed to fly into Ryoko's arms and cry on her shoulder. No, not that! She clapped herself on the head. *Mustn't lean on her now,* she told herself. *High time you stood on your own two feet.*

"…and that's my story," she wound up, her face flushed and wet with sweat and tears. She got up to make a fresh pot of tea.

Ryoko grunting. The click of the gas stove igniting. Sounds of the old tea being discarded, new tea leaves settling in. Ryoko staring grimly out the window.

"Leave him!" Ryoko yelled, then reconsidered: "You've got Hideto. I'll teach the bastard a lesson." Her tone was resolute.

Fiddling with the lid on the teapot filled with hot water, Sakiko looked at Ryoko. Should she say "Yes, please do," or "Never mind, I'll take care of it"? She couldn't decide.

Sensing Sakiko's state of frozen indecisiveness, Ryoko was perplexed. Eyes fixed on the *yokan* on the table, she crossed her arms firmly and didn't budge.

The little girl inside Sakiko suddenly came to life. And made a request: *Don't run away. If you do, both Hideto and I will be hurt. Be brave, be grown up.*

She took her hand off the teapot lid, laid her fingertips on the table, looked Ryoko in the eye and said, "I'll do it myself."

"Huh?"

Ryoko was on the verge of saying something with great force when her gaze and Sakiko's collided, intertwined, communed.

"What's happened?" Ryoko asked.

"I'm going to change," Sakiko answered. "I'm going to change myself!"

Had she put her foot in it? Despite having made the announcement to Ryoko, she couldn't quite execute her plan—and not for lack of opportunity. Paul was definitely spending more time at home. After Hideto went to sleep, he would wander around as if waiting for something. Had Ryoko said something to him? Maybe so—the realization deflated her. She felt like a daughter seeking to become independent, frustrated by her mother's attempts to help.

Ryoko never confronted her and asked if she'd talked to him. It was odd of her not to bring it up at all. Sakiko felt as though she were being watched. Still, the thought that someone cared filled her with warmth.

And Hideto's condition was getting worse. It was now or never.

Choosing a place where if they spoke in loud voices they would wake the sleeping Hideto, Sakiko sat down face to face with Paul. Here she would be able to control her emotions. Her heart was beating painfully fast. Toying with the wineglass in his hands, Paul waited for her to start talking. *Calmly, calmly,* she told herself, and began.

"You and Hiroko. I know all about it." Her voice and her body were shaking.

"No woman has any business telling a man what to do!" A memory arose in her mind of her father, Morimasa, his face purple-veined with anger as he thundered sternly. She tugged hard on an earlobe, shut her eyes, and chanted silently, *Go away.* The vision faded.

Paul fell still and stared at his hands. Several seconds went by. He set his wineglass on the table and sat unmoving, his head tipped to one side. His gaze rested somewhere in space. What was he plotting? Sakiko grew suspicious.

Then all at once he started to talk. With the air of someone who forgot to pick up his change, he said, "Oh yeah, that." As if to say, *I've got to go back and pick up my change, but let me say something first.*

"It happened. Didn't mean anything. That's how artists are made. It's your job as my wife to understand my nature and submit to it. You can't do secretarial work or entertain the way my friends' wives can. You're not a professional artist's wife. But I make the best of it."

You go get the change I forgot. Continuing in this vein, he said, "So I wish you wouldn't raise a fuss just because I had a little change of air."

Clearly he expected her to nod. His next words were on the tip of his tongue. To shove them back down his throat, she spoke up.

"If you call an affair with your wife's sister a 'change of air,' you're not normal."

His retort was lightning quick. "Artists aren't normal. That's what makes us artists." He wore a roguish smile that said, *Well? Clever and charming, aren't I?* Confronted by her icy gaze, he put on a droll look of surprise.

"Stop making fun," she said crisply.

"Okay." He straightened up, rolled his head to stretch his neck muscles, folded his arms. *Let's have it,* his posture said.

Now what should she do? Sakiko pressed her lips together, tightened her mouth, and let out a deep breath through her nose.

"I…I…"

Paul's look was inviting. *Go on, I won't be angry.*

"I've always gone along with other people's opinions and tried to give people what they wanted. I was afraid of not being liked, or of giving offense. My inability to say no has caused everyone a lot of trouble—especially Hideto. It hasn't been good for him at all."

The words spilled out, and Paul listened carefully, as if scooping them up one by one.

"As you advised me to do, I want to grow up. I'll try to express my own will and learn to say no. After all, the one who suffers the most if I don't is me myself."

Paul cut in before she could find the words to go on. "Good for you. I'll do all I can to help. I support you."

She glared at him a little, telling him to wait. He put a finger to his lips as if to say "Oops."

"Thank you for your support," she said. "But…" She faltered. Paul waited, seeming to hold back a stream of things he wanted to say.

"But I can't forgive you for what you did with my sister." She waited a beat, then looked him in the eye and said sincerely, her tone neither heavy nor light, "I want to end it."

"You what?"

"I said I want to end it."

"Our marriage?"

"Yes."

Sakiko looked at the space on the wall where the painting *Hiroko* had hung, and where now only the strut remained. A space that till now her eyes had avoided out of fear, as if an arm might come poking out and drag from her the awful memories she was suppressing.

There was the sound of Paul rubbing the tip of his finger along the edge of his wineglass. A sign he was deep in thought.

After a bit he put his palms together as if in prayer and said in a voice that rang with sincerity, "Sakiko, I'm sorry I hurt you. I apologize."

She lifted her face and looked at him. Mistakenly assuming she had accepted his apology, he smiled in relief. As their gazes collided, she said again, "I can't forgive what you did," and he, misunderstanding, said "Thank you." His smile turned to a grin.

"But Hiroko just happened to be your sister. What if it was someone else?"

"I know about your affairs with women. That has hurt me deeply too. But I relied on you, depended on you so much, I was afraid to leave you."

"And now because Hideto's having problems you've found the courage to leave me?"

"That definitely pushed me, but my sister is the main reason. Our divorcing won't be good for Hideto, but it would be worse if I stayed with you feeling this way."

"Wouldn't it be better if you became independent with my support?"

"That wouldn't work. I don't blame you for what happened with my sister, and here's why: you are a sick man where women are concerned. There's no point in blaming someone who is sick."

Paul's eyes gleamed as if to say *Aha! Now I've got you.* "So you'd walk away and leave a sick man? That's unfeeling of you."

"Your sickness is emotional. You've got to accept that and take steps to cure yourself. No one else can do that for you."

"I support your independence. Why not support me getting treatment for my sickness?" He said this as a stopgap, as if he did not believe for a minute that he was really sick.

"That's no good. There's too great a chance we'd pull each other down."

Paul started to laugh. Then he came up behind her, wrapped his arms around her and whispered, "You're funny today. Seeing you like this makes me love you all the more."

Quietly she disentangled herself and turned to face him. Looking straight into those blue eyes with black depths so charming she wanted to lose herself in them, she spoke:

"I can say only one thing: No."

"Daddy and Mommy have something to tell you," Sakiko said to Hideto. She could feel him grow tense, as if her tension had spread to him. She pulled him close and hugged him. Their two bodies were so rigid that it almost seemed they would rub together with a bristling sound. Reluctantly, his mouth pursed, Hideto went out on the terrace where Paul was, under the avocado tree.

Hideto sat between Sakiko and Paul. As he plopped down in the chair, Paul put an arm around his shoulders, patted him, and looked in his face with a smile. The gesture was completely natural. Probably his father had done the same to him when he was a boy. Sakiko was jealous; she wanted to try it, too.

"What we have to say is important," she said. "Mommy will talk first, and if you want to ask me anything, go right ahead. If you feel surprised or sad or upset, you can let your feelings out. You can hit us if you want, or you can cry. Daddy and Mommy can take it."

The words came out smoothly, with feeling. If she had gotten stuck or faltered midway, Paul had been poised to take over. He looked a bit let down.

Sakiko's delivery was smooth because she had acquired the English language away from her family. While speaking Japanese, memories brought her up short, making such pronouncements difficult.

Hideto was looking at her in wonder. For once, Mommy was trying to communicate with him. What for? Looking into his brown eyes, she wrapped her hands around his little ones and went on.

"Daddy and Mommy have decided to live separately. We tried hard, but we realized it's better if we don't live together."

"What'll happen to me?" Hideto's fearful voice cut in.

Who do you want to be with, she almost asked, but realized it was too abrupt.

"Mommy wants to live with you. So does Daddy. So all you have to do is choose what you want to do. We'll both respect your choice. We won't be at all jealous or resentful, I promise."

With his hands still in hers, Hideto looked at his parents in bewilderment.

"Is it hard?" asked Paul.

"You don't have to answer now," she said. "Take your time

and think about it." Her heart was pounding so loud she was afraid they could hear it. Cautiously she withdrew one hand and pretended to rub her shoulder. Paul glanced at her and took this as his cue.

"Today Mommy is learning ways to communicate, so I planned to keep quiet as much as possible, but I'll just tell you something important, okay? I'm telling you this just in case you might get the wrong idea. Our decision to live apart isn't your fault. Not one tiny little bit. It's just between Daddy and Mommy. So don't think it's because you did something you shouldn't have, or because you're bad, or anything like that. Not at all. If you ever have any thoughts like that, or if you ever feel that way—or if you have anything at all on your mind, I want you to tell us, either Daddy or Mommy or both. This is really important, okay?"

A ray of sunlight like a silver blade lit up Hideto's anxious face, and he gave a small nod. Watching, Sakiko saw her own childhood self superimposed on him. Staring at the two children standing in the sun, Hideto and little Sakiko, she smiled encouragingly.

"I want to live with Mommy."

Hideto's clear, unwavering voice struck an avocado over her head and ricocheted down on her ears.

"Really?" cried Paul, sounding so flustered that she couldn't help smiling. He frowned at her and said, "That's right, Mommy's better. Daddy's always working, so he can't take care of you properly. You get that, don't you?"

He hugged Hideto tight. The boy relaxed in his arms, then pulled away and said flatly, "I want to live in this house with Mommy. I don't want to leave my friends at school. No matter what."

"All right. That's what we'll do, then."

Hideto had expressed himself clearly for once. Sakiko, to

whom his feelings were painfully understandable, made a resolution: She would get a job and pay back the loan on the house. Paul's income alone wouldn't be enough to keep up separate households.

Paul was staring at her as if trying to read her mind.

What are you going to do, his eyes asked.

In his expression, sincere concern alternated with scorn at the idea that there was anything she could do.

"If Mommy says so, then there's nothing to worry about. Daddy will help, too."

There was something facetious in his tone. Hideto's anxiety swelled before her eyes. She glared at Paul. He looked away. He studied the lone avocado as if transforming it to some astronomical figure.

Nothing to worry about he had said, but she felt utterly forlorn. Could she possibly work, and raise this child, and build a life all on her own? *What'll happen to us?* As if sensing her thoughts, Hideto stared at her with a look like that of a leaf in a hurricane. She grabbed him and hugged him, and whispered with all the love she could muster: "It's okay. Mommy's going to be different from now on. She'll be so strong and dependable, you'll be surprised. So relax. Mommy and Daddy will still be friends, too. In fact we'll be better friends than ever, I know. So don't worry. Everybody's on your side."

Dear Mother and Father

I'm sorry it's been so long since I last wrote. I trust you are both well. Please forgive the suddenness of this letter. I really ought to go back to Japan and tell you in person, but circumstances make that impossible, so I must do it by letter instead. Once again, I ask your forgiveness.

Paul and I are getting a divorce.

I married without consulting you, and now I am divorcing without consulting you. I can well imagine how furious you must be. I offer heartfelt apologies.

The other day, we finalized the arrangements through our lawyers. Hideto will go on living with me in this house, and Paul will pay for childcare and monthly expenses. Hideto will spend every other weekend with him.

The arrangements may seem strange, given Japanese customs, but over here this is typical. So we will continue to be provided for, and my relationship with Paul is amicable, so please do not worry.

Take good care of yourselves.

Until now, whenever something came up Sakiko had contacted Eiko or the now-retired Miss Yamane, and they had conveyed the information to her parents on her behalf. This was the first letter she had ever written to her parents. She couldn't help imagining the look of mockery and admonition in the eyes of her father, Morimasa—a look of darkness so unfathomable that those on its receiving end all but lost their will to live.

"Who are you writing to, Mommy, that makes you look so scared?" Hideto came up to her now and then to peer at the Japanese writing as if it were something strange.

"I'm writing a letter to your grandfather and grandmother in Japan, but it's hard," she said.

"It's not hard for me to write letters to you and Daddy."

"That makes Mommy very happy."

She drew him close and kissed his plump cheek. The three

of them had had their talk, and since then there had been lots more communication. As a result, Hideto's infantile regression seemed to have stopped. He used to be skin and bones, so skinny that the old Fusako would surely have made fun of him, but he had filled out nicely and it no longer gave Sakiko a pang to embrace him.

She returned to the letter. Her wastebasket filled so quickly with crumpled stationery that she replaced it with a big garbage can. Somehow she managed to finish the task.

To help defray costs, she was going to do office work at a company run by a Japanese-American, a job that Ryoko had found for her, but this bit of information she did not include in the letter. Once her father knew she was short of money he would undoubtedly wire her some, and she didn't want him to.

Morimasa's reply came in the mail. As usual, he wrote on fine handmade paper, the brushstrokes forceful and calm.

> So you've gotten a divorce, have you? Raise your son with affection and care, and pay attention to your own health. If you ever need anything, don't hesitate to ask.

She read the letter standing in bright yellow-orange sunshine on the flagstone path between the mailbox and the front door. Her tears fell on the handmade paper, soaked in, and disappeared. Something in the texture of the paper made her feel it wouldn't be long now before she talked to her father.

From her mother there was no word. Eiko wrote instead.

> Father blames me for raising you badly, and Mother is absolutely wild. She moans about it to me constantly, so

199

thank you very much. There's a new expression nowa-
days, "full-time housewife." People think someone like me,
a stay-at-home wife and mother, has nothing to do all day,
but I am quite busy.

Write a letter to Mother with a proper apology that shows
some reflection on your part.

Everyone is relieved that you're not coming back to Japan and
bringing Hideto with you. Things won't be easy, but you've
made your bed, so now you've got to lie in it. Please don't be
under any illusion that there is anything to be gained by
coming back to Japan. Nobody here is expecting you.

The rest of the letter consisted of her boasting about her children

"I want to go to Japan," said Hideto after school one day. During class they had talked about each other's roots, and his classmates and teacher had been surprised to hear that although Hideto had been out East to see his paternal grandparents, he had never been to Japan. When Sakiko married Paul, the letter she received from Eiko telling her not to come back had made a strong impression on her, and she had vowed never to return. The topic of a trip to Japan had not arisen since.

Hideto's desire swayed her. She wanted to show him the country where his roots were; she wanted him to meet his Japanese relatives. She wrote a letter to Eiko mentioning that she was considering a trip to Japan.

Eiko wrote back.

It's better for everyone if you don't come. I haven't said any-
thing to Father yet, but Mother is in a state of shock and

confusion. You know her as well as I do, so you realize she never says what she thinks, but from the face she made, as if she had heard something unpleasant, I felt keenly that she wants you to abandon the idea.

Fusako and I are busy taking care of our own families, and Fusako says you haven't changed at all, that you are an egotistical person with no thought for the convenience of others. She's quite angry.

Furthermore, and this is not easy to write, I worry that what with one thing and another you will take it into your head to settle here in Japan. You probably have no intention of doing this, but when Hideto meets his cousins there is no telling what he may say. Besides, now that you and Paul are divorced, you have nothing to go back to in the United States, and financially you would be better off staying here. Even if you have no intention of relying on Father (I am giving you the benefit of the doubt here, be grateful), he will naturally offer to help. As far as that goes, the rest of us can't have you living like a pauper either. As a family we do have to keep up appearances.

You were the baby of the family, and we protected you growing up, so you have no idea what a scary place the world really is. It has probably never crossed your mind how much trouble you have caused your family, first by marrying Paul and now by divorcing him. Who can blame Fusako for being angry with you?

Let me just say, people are swayed by their surroundings. And they always choose the easier course. Having raised you since you were a little girl, I know very well that you, especially, are like that. Really. In fact, I can just about guarantee it.

Now do you understand why I don't want you to come back?

"Nope, makes no sense to me," Sakiko said under her breath with a wry smile. How typical of Eiko, to write only her worst forebodings.

Sakiko's reply:

I understand your point of view very well. However, this does not alter my wish to pay a visit. It is important for Hideto to be able to meet my family. Encountering the country and culture of Japan will be a good experience for him, perhaps even a necessary one. Here in this country, where so many different races live together, one becomes conscious of blood. The blood of one's ancestors. The bloodstream that has been passed down in the family, in the race, for generations. The meaning of that bloodstream is surprisingly great. I want Hideto to meet family members who share his blood. That is the source of a family's energy, too.

In case you are worried about where we will stay, we will be in a hotel, so it's all right. We won't cause you any trouble.

There is no chance whatever that we will stay on in Japan. Hideto is completely American, of course, and I've been Americanized too. Life here is easier for us. I solemnly swear that we will not cause you any trouble. I only hope that we can all get together.

One week later, there was a phone call from Fusako.

"I read your letter. Enough is enough. Going on about God

knows what—blood this, blood that—it gave me the creeps. Are you trying to speak in riddles? You can't fool me."

Nothing had changed, neither Fusako's menacing tone nor Sakiko's cowering.

"Look, when I say don't come, you don't come! Understand? Just shut up about it or you'll be sorry. And just because you've been living over there, don't get on your high horse. America is nothing but a land of immigrants, after all. Compare that to Japan—a race of superior people with *yamatodamashi,* the Japanese spirit."

Sakiko remembered hearing their father talk about this when she was a child.

"So listen to me. Having an emigrant like you come back to stay with us is a huge inconvenience. We have the family name to think of, you know. If we were any ordinary family, it wouldn't matter so much, but our family is different."

Sakiko worked up her courage and said, "Fusako, let me say something." Her voice rang out and then faded away, to no avail. Yet it seemed that a fragment of what she'd said hit Fusako's eardrums after all.

"What? What is it?" Her voice was hard, with a tremor.

Sakiko took a deep breath and said in one fluid speech, "Don't worry. Just imagine that some old friends of yours are coming home to Japan for a short visit and want to get together. Well, coming home isn't the right expression, I mean paying a visit…"

Fusako's sharp voice cut in. "That's absurd. Do you really think that sisters can meet, and treat each other as no more than friends? You always did say funny things. I see that hasn't changed."

Sakiko closed her eyes, focused her thoughts in the dark, regulated her breathing. *Give up,* said a low voice in her left ear, and *Don't give up,* said a low voice in her right ear, the two voices alternating. Quieting them down, she said, "I didn't express myself well. I'm sorry. What I meant to say is that even if we are sisters, we can maintain a certain distance, the way friends do."

Silence continued for about as long as it would take to cross a two-lane street. Then, in a tone of mingled uncertainty and irritation, Fusako said, "Well, you put me on the spot when you talk about standing on ceremony like that. Anyway, knowing you, I suppose you'll come no matter what anyone says."

She paused. Sakiko waited.

"Oh, all right. But promise you won't cause any trouble while you're here. If you break your promise, you'll be sorry!"

"I promise."

The receiver slammed down, as if to immobilize Sakiko's intimidated voice.

Her adrenaline racing, Sakiko felt a fleeting pang of regret. It made her uneasy that she had angered her sister. She knew better than anyone the destructive power of Fusako's anger. The sound of Fusako's emphatic "You'll be sorry!" lingered in her ears, sending her into a daze.

Paul's beat-up station wagon pulled up in front of the house, its engine chugging loudly, and came to a stop. He was here to pick up Hideto for the weekend. As he stuck one leg out of the car he asked Sakiko, who was pulling weeds as she waited, "Did something happen?"

She told him the details of the phone conversation with Fusako, and let him know that she was hesitating over whether or not to go. He laid his hands firmly on her shoulders, aware that she was fighting the impulse to have him make the decision for her. "Are you going to go forward or back?" he said. "Change yourself, or go back to being the way you were? You're the one who has to decide, Sakiko. Otherwise what was the whole point of our getting this divorce you wanted?"

"I know, but…" She swallowed the words she'd been about to say, but she was at her wits' end. Fusako's voice eddying in the receiver had confronted her with the reality of what waited in Japan, leaving her more terrified than if she were heading into some unknown, remote frontier.

Paul looked now up at the clear blue sky, now down the street at the rows of English-style houses ringed with roses, letting her know that the decision was hers and hers alone to make.

Sakiko stood with her feet planted firmly on the ground, sensing that she was anchored, and told herself over and over, in every way she could think of, to have self-confidence.

Hideto came flying out of the house with his knapsack, packed with all the clothes, books and things he would need for the weekend.

"Daddy, did you get the tickets to the game?"

"Yup, got 'em right here," Paul said, patting his jeans pocket.

"We're going to Japan!" Hideto said, his voice eager.

"That's great. I bet you'll have a helluva trip." With one arm around Hideto, Paul winked at Sakiko.

As she watched the car with the two of them in it disappear into the distance, Sakiko made up her mind: they would go to Japan. True, the impetus had come from Hideto, but in the end it was her decision. *This is good,* she told herself, nodding. *You passed the test.*

10 Some Things Change, Some Never Do

Standing in front of the zelkova gate, Hideto said, "This is like a samurai movie, huh."

They went through the door at the side of the gate. A moist gravel walkway led to the entrance, where there was a weeping cherry tree, enchantingly graceful in form. Sakiko was surprised to see how big it had grown.

When they went in the front door, her mother, Sadako, appeared and let out a small breath at the sight of them, then quickly said "Welcome!" to cover any awkwardness. Her eyes rested on Hideto and smiled, crinkling at the corners. Hideto looked his grandmother straight in the eye and greeted her in flawless Japanese without a trace of an accent. The intensive work he'd done on his Japanese, once they decided they were going, had paid off. Sadako responded with a slight tilt of the head.

They followed Sadako down a hallway of polished pine.

The scuffling of Hideto's slippers underscored for Sakiko the distance between California and this world. It shocked her to see how the years had shrunk her mother and rounded her back. She regretted having stayed away for nearly two decades.

To the right was the family's everyday living space. At the end of the hallway, on the left, was the reception room, where Sadako showed them in.

A large room with a rosewood table; a garden containing a weathered lantern from the Kamakura era, ending in a low, white stone wall with a tile roof. Cherry trees in the distance added to the view. Returning her gaze inside, Sakiko realized that the air conditioner was hidden in a tasteful wooden casing with only a low hum to give its presence away.

Her mother waited until the two of them were seated on floor cushions before leaving the room.

Through the insistent trilling of cicadas came the resonant clack of a *shishi-odoshi,* a length of bamboo that slowly filled with water and hit against a stone each time it emptied. She wondered if the gardener still came every day. Her eyes searched the well-cared-for garden for his figure. Today was the fourth day since their arrival in Japan, and Hideto, who had shown curiosity about everything, seemed astonished by this classically Japanese house. A maid brought in tea and cake. The teacups were elegant, gold-rimmed with a floral design of pale green. Sadako's taste remained unerring.

"Mommy," Hideto said in English, "You're nervous." It was as if he had opened his knapsack and let out a burst of dry, fresh California air. Sakiko smiled and raised her teacup to her lips. Her hand shook ever so slightly.

Eiko, wearing a white blouse and a navy knee-length skirt, came striding in, accompanied by a girl who looked somehow cowed. The girl was overshadowed by her mother, just as the four sisters had always been overshadowed by theirs.

"Hello," said Eiko. "You're looking good." Something in her gaze suggested a mother assessing her child. She prodded the girl standing silently beside her. "Momoko, this is your Aunt Sakiko. What do you say?"

Like a mechanical doll that had been switched on, Momoko abruptly dropped to the floor and bent over till her forehead nearly touched the tatami floor. "How do you do," she chirped.

"Ugh! Can't you be more graceful?" Disgusted with her daughter's failure to live up to expectations, Eiko glared at her with undisguised ill humor. The habit was all too vivid in Sakiko's memory.

Eiko then shone a bright smile on Hideto. "You're Hideto. You must teach Momoko English." Her tone was firm, commanding.

"Of course," Hideto answered in English, apparently flustered since this wasn't how he had imagined meeting his relatives in Japan. He got up and held out his hand, forgetting what he had been taught: in Japan you don't shake hands, you bow.

"Oh, a handshake! So you are an American after all. All right then." She gripped his hand so hard she startled him, successfully conveying the message, *Go against me and you'll be sorry.*

Brisk footsteps sounded in the hallway, and Fusako appeared, pausing just outside the threshold. "Hello. Hideto, we're so glad you could come." Turning to a little girl with braids standing behind her, she said in a commanding voice, "Come on, Kanako." She stood erect with dignity, shoulders back and chest out, wearing a light summer sweater with a pattern of bright red roses. Sakiko found her impressive.

Glancing at Sakiko as if she vaguely recalled who she might be, Fusako said, "Thanks for coming in all this heat." As she spoke, she crossed the room and stepped out on the veranda. Sliding one of the glass doors several inches open, she stuck her head out and looked around the garden. "Just look how they cut the grass," she clucked disapprovingly, gazing down at the lawn. "Not very chic."

"Close the door, Fusako, you're letting in hot air."

At Eiko's impatient voice, Fusako turned her shoulders in her sister's direction to indicate she had heard, and went on inspecting the garden.

Kanako and Momoko sat talking in whispers, darting quick glances at Hideto. Sadako looked fondly at her grandchildren.

There was a stir in the hallway, and Morimasa appeared, wearing an elegant kimono of dark-blue silk.

"Fusako!" Though low, Eiko's voice was tense enough to bounce off the glass door. Fusako shut the door with such haste that she pinched her finger. She put her fingertip in her mouth and took it out again, erased the frown from her face, then came in and sat down as if nothing had happened.

Morimasa seated himself in front of the alcove, where there hung a scroll painting by the seventeenth-century Zen monk Hakuin. He held himself ramrod straight, lifted his irritable face and looked at them all. Despite having promised herself she would look him in the eye, Sakiko dropped her gaze. Silence and tension filled the room.

Morimasa's eyes came to Hideto, and he said in a voice of clarity and strength, "Welcome. Thank you for coming such a long way to see us."

"*Ojiisama, konnichiwa.*" Grandfather, hello. Hideto looked straight at his grandfather as he greeted him. His grandfather returned his gaze, and smiled.

After a beat, Morimasa turned slowly to Sakiko. "Sakiko, it's you…" His mouth trembled slightly, and moisture dimmed the gleam in his age-hollowed eyes.

"Father," said Sakiko, "forgive me. I'm sorry I made you worry." That was all she could manage. Over her head, as she laid her hands one on top of the other and leaned over till her forehead touched the tatami mat, the air seemed to freeze.

"That's enough, that's enough."

Cautiously raising her head at the sound of her father's warm voice, she saw gentleness in his eyes, the gentleness of someone who has accepted a life of trials.

The rest of the family seemed to feel awkward and uncomfortable. Fusako sent the silent message, *Don't blame me. What on earth were you thinking?* Sadako hung her head and trembled visibly, fearful that later on Morimasa's anger would explode in her face as he accused her of failing to raise Sakiko properly.

The maid brought in a tray of fine black pine bearing teacups of Kokaratsu ware. "Thank you," Morimasa said. The maid looked at him, her face glowing with joy. The entire family wanted to speak to Morimasa that way, face to face, but they could not. Envy and discontent filled the air.

There was a rustle of silk as Morimasa folded his arms and closed his eyes. Each family member made a surreptitious gesture of exploration, taking care not to intrude on the world behind his closed lids. They reached out and briefly touched their lacquer saucer for no reason, or patted their face with a handkerchief, their movements furtive and clumsy.

Morimasa's eyelids twitched. Everyone started. Fusako glared at Momoko and Kanako, who were quietly poking each other. From Eiko's vicinity came the sound of someone taking a deep and circumspect breath.

"Momoko, Kanako, how have you been?" Morimasa's voice rang out all of a sudden, nearly making them jump in surprise. He sounded as if he had been turning something over in his mind and had come to some private conclusion.

The two girls were too flustered to speak. Their mothers, Eiko and Fusako, shot fiercely reprimanding looks at them. The looks met and clashed midway, giving off sparks.

Morimasa closed his eyes again.

"Momoko!" Eiko urged, in a voice that sounded muddy, as if it had welled up from the bowels of the earth. "Yes. I am fine," said the girl. She sounded like a soldier responding to his superior officer; it was hard to tell if the words were meant for her grandfather or her mother.

"Answer your grandfather properly!" Eiko insisted tightly. Momoko was trembling, her very blood turning to ice in her veins. Sakiko saw her old self in the girl.

"That will do, Eiko," Morimasa said reprovingly. Then he turned to his granddaughters. "I see. You'll be needing some spending money, I suppose." Though mindful of their mothers, the girls exchanged delighted looks.

Hideto's eyes darted about the room, animated with curiosity—almost as if he were watching actors at a dress rehearsal. Observing his behavior, Morimasa asked him a series of questions—how old was he, did he have any friends, what did he like to do—nodding and making appreciative comments at the boy's replies in halting Japanese. He turned to Sakiko.

"Use Japanese at home. The boy is bright; he'll pick it up in no time."

"Yes, I'll do that." She looked directly at her father as she replied, and after a moment's hesitation, added, "Father..." Her heart shook, her voice quavered, her throat constricted. Words wouldn't come. Chill air seeped from the others in the room, as if they had turned to frozen trees. The silence was so profound she could hear leaves flutter from the treetops.

The little girl inside Sakiko stirred. Then posed a question. *Isn't this the time? The time to realize your long-cherished goal?*

Mustering all her strength, Sakiko said, "Father, you've been to the United States. What did you think of it?"

"I thought it was full of energy."

"I like that about it, too."

"Is that right?"

"Did you ever go to Los Angeles?"

"An old friend of mine lives there. He came to the airport to meet me, took one look at my face and called me by my old nickname: 'Mo!' There were tears in his eyes." Her father's own eyes misted at the recollection. "It was a nice, sunny place. That's where you live, isn't it?"

For the first time in her life, Sakiko enjoyed a meandering conversation with her father. She spoke to him calmly and without restraint; he smiled, responded to her questions, sometimes shook with laughter, even showed surprise. Just like Mii-chan and her father long ago.

Her father's black look of scorn and reproach, that look that she had lived in fear and dread of for so long, would never again cross her mind. It was as if a mental projector had been smashed.

Cutting through the black eddies of jealousy emitted by her mother and sisters, Hideto sent her a look of encouragement.

Her father said, "If there's anything you need, any sort of problem, just say so. I don't know where you're staying...you should stay here."

Without raising her head or breaking her silence, Sadako exuded opposition with every fiber of her being. Understanding, Morimasa got up with a look of resignation and left, accompanied by a maid. He paused at the threshold, turned, and said to Sakiko and Hideto, "Come again." His voice trembled ever so slightly.

As if she had been waiting impatiently for Morimasa's figure to disappear into the dimness of the hallway, Fusako turned to Sakiko. "Why of all times did you have to pick this time of year to come?" she demanded. "Thanks to you, we had to come back to Tokyo in this god-awful heat. You never did think about anybody but yourself."

"I'm sorry. We wanted to come sooner, but Hideto had camp…"

"Camp!" Fusako's shrill voice rang out in scorn and disbelief.

Picking up on their mother's concern that others might overhear, Eiko raised her chin, intending to rein her sister in, but was overwhelmed by the other's burst of energy.

"Camp is just playtime! Why in God's name would you send him to camp knowing it would cause trouble for us? In the first place, you, you…." Tripping over her own words, Fusako let the sentence die.

When Morimasa left the room, Sakiko had relaxed her formal posture, but now she sat bolt upright again. Making eye contact with the others one by one, she said, "I apologize for causing trouble. I'm really sorry. I hate to make excuses, but Hideto had a long-standing promise to go to camp with his friends, and I wanted him to be able to keep his promise."

"You can't let a child dictate to you what to do. Is that how you run things at your house? Why not show him who's boss?" Fusako spoke sharply, having regained her balance.

"Of course I say no when I have to. But I don't do it to show him who's boss, I do it because he needs to know what's appropriate and what isn't. This time, he and I talked it over, and I realized how important the promise was to him, so I respected his wishes. As a result I ended up causing you all trouble, for which I sincerely apologize."

"What kind of a way is that to talk? Listen to her, what a smart mouth she's got. Honestly…it makes me so mad…"

When Fusako had quieted down a little, Eiko interceded. "We're all together for the first time in so long. Let's make an effort, shall we?"

Relieved, their mother sent Eiko a grateful look. Pride shone in Eiko's eyes; she straightened her back. "Lunch will be grilled eel, Yukihiko's favorite," she said. "Serves him right for not coming. Now that he's in college, friends come before family. No sense of duty to his parents at all. Sakiko, you'd better prepare yourself."

Hideto had never tried eel before. Curious, he took a mouthful, then wrinkled his nose and hastily swallowed it down without chewing. Everybody laughed. Fusako instantly said, "He's never had eel? Poor thing!" Momoko and Kanako laughed covertly, each with a hand covering her mouth, and Eiko flashed them a disapproving glance.

"Shall we order something else for him?" asked Sadako sympathetically.

"Whatever you've got on hand would be fine," said Sakiko. "Eggs or something. He can eat the rice."

"We could order sushi."

"The poor child has probably never had that, either," said Fusako with a thin smile.

"Sushi's popular in America, so it's easy to get. Hideto likes it, too." She turned to Hideto and asked him what he wanted. Momoko and Kanako gasped and quickly turned to their mothers to see their reaction.

"Never mind her. Around here, the mother has the last word." Fusako leaned forward, the diamond pendant around her neck dangling, and spoke to the girls emphatically. With every word, the pear-shaped diamond swung and sparkled as if to reflect her authority.

Sensing the drift of the conversation, Hideto said, "I'm hungry, so instead of waiting for sushi I'll have this rice. It's flavored with soy sauce, so it's good."

Sakiko translated. The words were no sooner out of her

mouth than Fusako sniffed, "Quite the little diplomat! A brilliant career awaits him no doubt. That is, unless you purposely mistranslated what he said." Her sister's quick thinking was impressive in its way, Sakiko thought. If only Fusako could find a way to put that skill to use in society somehow.

"Why are you staying in that shabby excuse for a hotel?" This too from Fusako. "We've got the Morimoto name to consider, you know. It's important to keep up appearances."

Appearances—now there was a word Sakiko well remembered. The family was always concerned about appearances: *What will people say? What will they think?* That habit had been beaten into her from the time she was a little girl; she'd had a hard time getting rid of it. Was there still a remnant of it left in her? she wondered. Putting her fingertips to her chest as if in search of such a remnant, she said, "I'm sorry, but that is all I can afford. It's perfectly pleasant."

"Don't talk nonsense. You know very well if people find out you're staying in a cheap hotel, we are the ones who'll be embarrassed! How can you be so thick-headed?"

"I can't understand your way of thinking."

"Oh, no? Then by all means, let me explain." Fusako fixed her eyes on Sakiko as she spoke. "Money is a measuring stick. People with money have common sense. It's a sign they're safe, respectable...the chosen ones." She uttered the last words in a kind of trance. With a hand that bore a jade ring, she lifted her teacup, Old Imari ware from the seventeenth century, to her lips.

You're insane. The words were on the tip of Sakiko's tongue, but she bit them back, not wanting to spoil the occasion.

"Fusako," said Eiko, "that teacup is valuable, and it means a lot to Mother. Put it down."

The teacup was one that Sadako always washed herself, not letting the maids near it. Fusako carefully returned it to its lacquer saucer. Her anger at having been cautioned, and at herself for having complied, was then redirected at Sakiko.

"So you got divorced. Nice way to drag the family name in the mud. How are we supposed to hold our heads up in public now? Even an idiot like you must realize what you've done. Now if our children can't get married, what are you going to do about it? Are you prepared to take responsibility?"

Sadako turned pale. Eiko said to Momoko and Kanako, "Why don't you girls go show Hideto the photo albums?"

Eiko glared at Fusako, restraining her from saying more until the children had safely disappeared down the hallway. Then, after a pause, she turned to her mother. "Didn't you say you had a kimono you thought Momoko could wear? Would you let me see it?" Sadako had been sitting with her hands folded, looking down. The two of them got up and left the room.

Fusako had been watching and waiting impatiently, and as soon as the room was clear she burst out, "There's something I want to say to you about Hiroko. Why didn't you go?"

"You mean when she died?" Surprised at the unexpected turn in the conversation, Sakiko blurted out words she had wanted never to speak in this house.

"Yes, when she died."

The voice was bitter and heavy, overriding hers. Sakiko was dumbfounded by the malevolence in her sister's tone.

"Making Paul go in your place." Fusako's eyes were challenging, her mouth twisted in a slight smile.

Sakiko slowly breathed in and out before answering. "Paul took off without consulting me. I had Hideto, so I couldn't go chasing after him. Also, he knows the language and the customs better than I do, so I thought it would be better to leave it in his hands. And I was right."

"That's no excuse. You had people from the company there

to help you. You could have done it just as well. You should have. What do you suppose those people thought? Having her brother-in-law show up instead of her own sister."

"They said they were grateful."

"And you believed them! That's the trouble with aliens. That's all they could say, don't you see?"

The trilling of the cicadas, until then a pleasant reminder of summers past, now sounded abrasive in Sakiko's ears.

Looking off in the direction of the cherry trees, Fusako said with feigned casualness, "I know why you didn't go. You were jealous." She tittered.

Sakiko's body seemed to rise in the air. Her heart felt as if it would erupt. "I knew nothing about that until you sent me what she wrote." Her voice was strained.

"Well, pardon me! I was sure you knew about it long before. I just assumed you'd want to know the details. My intentions were the best.... And for my trouble I get a scolding?" Fusako looked at the teacup in her hands, smiling. Her full-cheeked face radiated dark delight.

Controlling her welling anger, Sakiko asked, "Fusako, what made you do such a thing?"

"Are you saying I shouldn't have? In that case I apologize. I must say you have thin skin."

"I was deeply hurt. What you did shows a lack of common sense. Just now you said that the rich have common sense, but you yourself are proof it's not true."

"What is this, a lecture? Spare me."

"And why talk to me like that?" said Sakiko. "It's sad…"

"Sad? Do you presume to feel sorry for me? You, feel sorry for me?" Fusako's voice was choked with anger.

"No, that's not what I meant. I don't know how to put it. I don't want to be at sword's point with you all the time. I just want to have a real conversation."

"I've got nothing to say to you," Fusako snorted.

"Then listen." Before Fusako could reply, Sakiko plunged on. She thought she understood how they had gotten to this point, and she wanted her sister to understand, too.

"Ever since I was a little girl, I've always felt you came down too hard on me. I tried to think why. Then I realized it had to do with the way we were brought up. We grew up in a family that was a family in name only. Maids looked after us, young girls living far from home in a strange house. They had to work from morning till night, and they were tired to the bone. It must have been hard on them, having to take care of babies when they were young and homesick themselves. And just when you got old enough to look after yourself, I came along—a new burden. They stopped paying attention to you. You must have gotten jealous and tried to take your resentment out on me. The tired young maids never stopped to think about your feelings, and just scolded you for being mean to me. You picked on me all the more. Mother never knew anything about it. So the twisted feelings you had about me are deeply rooted in your heart, I think, and have always shaped your attitude toward me."

"I have no idea what you're talking about!" Fusako's face was taut, and her voice burst out from between pale, bloodless lips. A voice that came from her very core. There was a short, bewildered silence, fraught with emotion.

"It's just like you to shift responsibility to the maids. Blame other people, that's what you always do. Honestly, if you knew how I've suffered from your vicious personality..." Fusako's exasperated voice caught in her throat.

Sakiko took a deep breath. "If I have caused you trouble, I'm sorry. But I don't think I have a vicious personality."

"Stop it, you conceited little shit!" There was a nastiness in her tone, as if she were scattering raw garbage.

"Nobody's to blame. It's our family. We were never a real family. That's why we ended up like this, a pair of sisters who are always off kilter and never able to communicate. Let's fix things between us. At least let's change the way we talk to each other."

"I haven't got time to sit here listening to your stupid lecture from on high," Fusako snapped, her mouth twisted. "We're all busy. Just go home."

From long habit, following dictates laid down in childhood, Sakiko's hand reached for her purse. But an inner voice asked, *Why? Why do you have to go home? Think for yourself, Sakiko.* She put her hand back in her lap. "I'm not leaving."

Fusako stared at her incredulously. Then she jumped up and cried, "Go home! You heard me!"

Sakiko's hand hovered over her purse, and pulled back again. Seeing the hostility and confusion in Fusako's eyes, Sakiko controlled the trembling of her lips and said firmly, "First I'll ask Mother and Eiko what they want me to do. If they want me to leave, I will. I won't put your wishes ahead of theirs."

"Go on home."

Ignoring her sister's repeated command, Sakiko got up, intending to look for her mother and Eiko. Before she could reach the door, Fusako caught her arm from behind.

"Oh, all right. I see what you're saying. Come here." Her voice was low and husky.

Never before had Fusako said such words to her. Sakiko turned, wrapped her arms around her sister tightly from behind, and whispered in her ear, "Let's get along."

Fusako nodded, or perhaps she didn't. Letting go of her, Sakiko swiftly crossed the room and slid open a glass door. The trilling of cicadas rushed in and surrounded her as if in praise. Her heart sang.

Endnote

There are a few points in the text that Western readers may not understand or be familiar with.

One is on page 41, where Hanako is left to carry on her father's name. This would have been through the centuries-old tradition of *mukoyoshi* (adopted son-in-law), by which a bridegroom took his bride's surname. The practice kept families with no male heir from dying out.

Another is the song on page 95. "Ringo no uta" (Apple Song) by Hachiro Sato and Tadashi Manjome, was the breakout song from a movie released on October 10, 1945, a month after Japan's formal surrender to the Allied forces. "I touch my lips to a red apple, / And the blue sky watches in silence. / The apple says nothing, / But I understand its feelings. / The apple is lovely, a lovely apple." The liberated, carefree mood of the lyrics helped make this song a huge hit in the early postwar years.

※

About the Author

Mako Idemitsu was born and raised in Tokyo, Japan, in an elite, conservative family. In 1963, she moved to the US, where she met and married abstract expressionist painter Sam Francis. Raising two children in California, she became disillusioned with her roles as wife and mother, and picked up an 8mm camera. She began making experimental films investigating gender, domesticity, and Japanese identity. Her artwork is critically acclaimed and featured in museums across the world. She currently lives in Tokyo with her Japanese husband.

About the Translator

Juliet Winters Carpenter studied Japanese literature at the University of Michigan and translation at the Inter-University Center for Japanese Language Studies in Tokyo. Her past translations include *Secret Rendezvous* by Abe Kobo, *Masks* by Fumiko Enchi, and the works of Minae Mizumura. In 2016, she became the first person to win the prestigious Japan-US Friendship Commission Prize for the Translation of Japanese Literature twice.